NAVY SEAL SIX PACK

New York Times Bestselling Author

ELLE JAMES

This book is dedicated to my editor, whom I adore, Patience Bloom, for all the love, care and feeding she gives me as an author. She's a pleasure to work with and a wonderful person. I wish her all the happiness in the world, because she brings me joy and happiness just by being who she is.

Recycling programs for this product may not exist in your area.

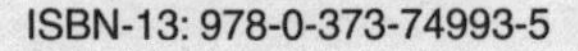

ISBN-13: 978-0-373-74993-5

Navy SEAL Six Pack

This edition published by arrangement with Harlequin Books S.A.

For questions and comments about the quality of this book, please contact us at CustomerService@Harlequin.com.

Printed in U.S.A.

Elle James, a *New York Times* bestselling author, started writing when her sister challenged her to write a romance novel. She has managed a full-time job and raised three wonderful children, and she and her husband even tried ranching exotic birds (ostriches, emus and rheas). Ask her, and she'll tell you what it's like to go toe-to-toe with an angry 350-pound bird! Elle loves to hear from fans at ellejames@earthlink.net or ellejames.com.

Books by Elle James

Harlequin Intrigue

SEAL of My Own

Navy SEAL Survival
Navy SEAL Captive
Navy SEAL to Die For
Navy SEAL Six Pack

Covert Cowboys, Inc.

Triggered
Taking Aim
Bodyguard Under Fire
Cowboy Resurrected
Navy SEAL Justice
Navy SEAL Newlywed
High Country Hideout
Clandestine Christmas

Visit the Author Profile page at Harlequin.com for more titles.

CAST OF CHARACTERS

Benjamin "Montana" Raines—Raised on a ranch in Montana, but trained as an expert sniper.

Kate McKenzie—Disgraced CIA special agent desperate to redeem herself.

Becca Smith—Stealth Operations Specialists (SOS) agent searching for the person responsible for her father's death.

Quentin Lovett—Navy SEAL, the charmer of the team.

Sawyer Houston—Navy SEAL gunner and secretly the son of a US Senator.

Dutton "Duff" Calloway—Navy SEAL trained demolitions expert and boat driver.

"Rip" Cord Schafer—Navy SEAL demolitions expert.

Jace Hunter—Newest member of Navy SEAL Boat Team 22.

Royce Fontaine—Head of the SOS.

Tim "Geek" Trainer—SOS agent with highly evolved computer skills.

Cassandra Teirney—Identity thief the SEAL team ran into in Cancun, spotted in DC.

Nigel Carruthers—Old friend and golfing buddy of deceased millionaire Trevor Brantley.

Tarek Abusaid—Syrian ambassador to the United States.

Mica Brantley—Trevor Brantley's widow, desperately searching for her stepdaughter.

Chapter One

Navy SEAL Benjamin "Montana" Raines leaned against the side of the nondescript building in downtown Washington, DC. Anyone looking at it would guess it was nothing more than another office building filled with businessmen or lobbyists there to buy a congressman or senator into their way of thinking.

Montana liked being outside, even if it was on a busy street in DC. He preferred the open air and big skies of his home state, Montana, but this city was a nice change from the heat, humidity and mosquitoes prevalent at his duty station in Stennis, Mississippi. Not that he minded Mississippi all that much. That little backwater town was home to the Pearl River and some of the best riverine training in the country.

For the past four years, Montana had been

with SEAL Boat Team 22, or as he and his team called it, SBT-22. The men on the team were more family than his own family back home. He'd been to hell and back with his fellow SEAL teammates and he'd give his life for each and every one of them.

Trained to conduct covert operations in river and jungle environments, Montana was feeling a bit out of his element and naked in DC. Instead of trees, brush and bugs, his surroundings consisted of concrete, cars and pavement. What bothered him most was that he couldn't openly carry a weapon, and he wasn't wearing any kind of protection—no Kevlar helmet or body armor. Civilian attire was the uniform of the day, with orders to try to look like he belonged in Washington, DC. Most of all, be on the lookout for his new partner.

His team had picked him for this operation because he was good at camouflage and he had experience with bombs. Whether it was in a desert, forest, golf course or city, he could blend in. From what he'd been told, his partner had similar skills. Which could be why he hadn't spotted her yet.

The need to blend in would be useful in a city where blending in normally wasn't the goal. Everyone in DC was, or wanted to be, someone. From the politicians always aware of the next election, to the lobbyists or leaders of the political action committees. All mingling with the rich and famous who hoped to manipulate the lawmakers with promises of campaign funding and vacations on fully staffed, luxury yachts.

None of that appealed to Montana. He'd rather be riding a horse on the prairie or staring up at the big sky on a starry night. He couldn't even see the stars in DC. The light pollution was off the scale and visible from the International Space Station like a gaudy jewel in a long chain of similarly gaudy jewels lining the East Coast.

A bicycle courier stopped on the sidewalk at the corner of the building Montana leaned against. The basket on the front of his bright yellow bicycle was overloaded with small packages and thick envelopes, precariously stacked. He toed the kickstand and dismounted. One by one, he removed the larger packages, lining them up against the building. Then he carefully rearranged them in the basket. A moment later he mounted his bicycle and rode off.

The courier passed Montana and crossed the street.

Montana glanced back the direction from

which the cyclist had come and frowned. A small package lay against the brick of the building.

Montana spun toward the cyclist and yelled, "Hey!"

The young courier either didn't hear him or ignored him, hurrying toward his next delivery. Which could have been to deliver the package he'd left behind. Already he was too far away to hear someone shouting at him over the sounds of the traffic on the street, or for Montana to catch him on foot.

Montana turned back to the package and walked toward it. Perhaps it had an address on it, or the phone number of the delivery service. He could call and have them send the courier back to retrieve it.

He had just about reached the package when a flash of motion made him look up in time to see a jean-clad female, with shoulder-length, straight blond hair, flying at him.

The crazy woman bent over and plowed into him, her shoulder hitting him square in his gut, sending him staggering backward. She didn't stop plowing until he'd been pushed several yards along the sidewalk, tripped over his feet and landed hard on his back. He lay still for a moment, the breath knocked out of his lungs, not only from the fall, but from the woman landing on top of him.

When he could drag a breath of air in to fill his lungs, he grabbed the woman's shoulders and pushed her to arm's length. "What the hell?"

"Stay down!" she shouted, and covered the back of her head with her arms, burying her face in his chest.

Not sure why he should keep down, he recognized the command in her voice and remained on the ground. He even threw his arm over his face.

Several seconds went by. People passed them on the sidewalk. A woman giggled, a man snorted and a child asked, "Mama, what's that woman doing to that man?"

"Shh," the woman said. "I'll tell you when you're older."

At that point, Montana opened his eyes and looked around. "Is something supposed to happen?"

His assailant leaned up on her arms and looked behind her. "The cyclist left a package. It could be full of explosives."

Montana chuckled. "Or it could be full of cookies, or paper clips, or someone's special-ordered dentures." He stared up into steely-gray eyes and studied the woman who'd tackled him. "Not that I mind letting the woman be on top, but I prefer it to be in the privacy of my bedroom, not a sidewalk crowded with people."

The female pushed to her feet and stared at the small box leaning against the side of the building, her eyes narrowed. "It could be a bomb," she said, as the bright yellow bicycle sailed past her.

Montana rose behind her, recognizing the cyclist from a few minutes earlier.

The rider barely came to a stop before he dropped to the ground and scooped up the box. Back on the bicycle, he jerked the handlebars around and sped away, hitting the street to weave in and out of the slow-moving traffic.

"Tragedy averted," Montana couldn't help saying. "Thank you for saving me from a fate worse than Grandma's cookies."

The woman stiffened, color rising in her cheeks. "Excuse me." With her chin lifted high enough that she couldn't possible see her feet, she marched away.

Montana resumed his post next to the entrance of the Stealth Operation Specialists headquarters, his gaze following the woman with the steely-gray eyes and sandy-blond hair.

She'd crossed the street and stopped to

stare at the numbers on the building in front of her. Performing an about-face, she retraced her steps and stopped in front of him to stare at the number on the outside of the building.

With a chuckle, Montana asked, "You wouldn't happen to be Kate McKenzie, would you?"

She closed her eyes briefly, then opened them and nodded. "I am."

"Since we already know each other on an intimate level, let me introduce myself. Benjamin Raines, but my friends call me Montana. I hear we're going to be partners."

KATE WANTED TO sink into the concrete sidewalk and die of mortification. Instead, she sucked it up and held out her hand as if she tackled perfect strangers on a regular occurrence. "Nice to meet you. I don't suppose you'd keep our little…incident to yourself, would you?"

"It'll be our secret." He took her hand, his strong, callused fingers wrapping around hers. She had no doubt he could crush her bones with one tight squeeze, if he wanted. A ripple of awareness feathered across her senses.

When she'd been lying on top of him, she'd felt the rock-hard muscles of his chest and thighs. He was built as solid as an armored tank. When her old college roommate, Becca, had briefed her on this mission, she'd told her she'd be paired with a Navy SEAL. The image in her mind had been one of a scruffy man with a beard and intense eyes. Not this ruggedly handsome, clean-shaven man wearing blue jeans, cowboy boots and a blue chambray shirt. He could have been a model for a jeans commercial, the kind of jeans best suited for horseback riding, not hanging out on street corners in the city.

"We've been waiting for you," he said, his voice deep and smooth like warm chocolate being poured over her skin, seeping into every crevice. "Come with me."

To the end of the earth. The thought leaped into her mind and she quickly banished it. Kate had more than proved herself a lousy judge of men and matters of the heart. But she couldn't stop the shiver that slipped down the back of her neck as she passed him and entered the building.

Montana led the way to the elevator and waited for her to enter before he punched a button on the panel.

As the car rose, Kate held her tongue. What could she say after making a complete fool of herself? "Do you know what this so-called mission is all about?"

Montana nodded but didn't enlighten her. While the elevator car rose, he leaned against the wall, studying her.

"I take it you're not going to clue me in." Kate hit him with a brief but unswerving glare, and then jerked her gaze away, avoiding direct eye contact, afraid of repeating her own history. Hadn't she fallen for a handsome colleague once before? Drawn into his world, his life, she'd been hard-pressed and embarrassed to admit she'd fallen for the oldest double cross in the book.

Maybe she deserved to be a desk jockey for the remainder of her career as a CIA special agent. Determined not to fall under any man's spell ever again, Kate watched the numbers blink on the display over the door. Two. Three.

A loud boom echoed in the air. The elevator jerked to a halt so suddenly Kate was thrown to her knees. Lights blinked out and absolute darkness descended on the enclosed box.

"Are you all right?" Montana's deep voice filled the abyss.

"Yeah." She pushed to her feet, bracing her hand on the wall. "What happened?"

"I think your bomb exploded."

No sooner had the words left his mouth than another explosion rocked the elevator and dust sifted through the air vent. Thrown sideways, Kate crashed into the hard body of the Navy SEAL.

His arm circled her waist, pulling her tightly against him.

Kate waited in silence, her chest crushed to his, listening for the next explosion, sounds of sirens or voices.

After a couple minutes and nothing else exploding, Kate broke her silence. "You can let go of me. I think that was the last one."

"We can't be sure," he said, his arm tightening, his fingers digging into the small of her back. "Give it another minute or two."

The longer she waited in the circle of his arm, her body absorbing his heat, the more time she had to take in just how tall and firm this man's body was. From what she'd felt, he didn't have an ounce of fat anywhere. And he smelled of outdoors and fresh air. She inhaled, deeply.

"You were right. It was the last one," he said, his breath stirring the loose strands of hair on her cheek. His arm loosened.

For a long moment, Kate remained pressed against him, her thoughts in a whirl, her blood hammering through her veins. Then she remembered to let go of the breath she'd been holding, and backed away. "I don't suppose you have a flash—"

A light blinked on in the darkness.

When her eyes adjusted to the sudden illumination, Kate shook her head. "You don't look like the kind of guy who carries a penlight."

Montana grinned. "I'm not. But Becca's boss gave me this one. It also contains a hidden camera. I might be a cowboy at heart, but the James Bond in me goes all techno-geek with stuff like this." He shined the light at the control panel. "Suppose the emergency button will work without electricity?"

"Only one way to find out." She pressed the button and waited. No sirens nor flashing lights came to life. She shrugged. "Help me pry the doors open so we can see where we are."

Montana placed the penlight between his teeth, dug his fingers between the sliding doors and pulled hard enough that Kate could get her fingers between, as well.

"On three," she said. "One…two…three."

They pulled hard in opposite directions. At first the door didn't budge much. Kate leaned back as hard as she could, digging her feet into the floor for leverage. Inch by hard-earned inch, the door opened, until there was enough room for one of them to squeeze through.

Montana shone the light, starting at their feet. The dark wall of the elevator shaft stared back at them. He swept the beam of light upward to the top, where they could see a four-inch gap to what Kate assumed was the fourth floor.

Montana gave her a sideways glance. “You don’t suppose you could fit through?”

She shook her head. “I’m smaller than you, but I’d have to be a cat to squeeze through that narrow gap.”

Montana trained the light at the ceiling of the car. “Then there’s only one other way out of here. Here, hold the flashlight.” He handed it to her, cupped his hands and bent down. “Check it out.”

She stared at his cupped hands and didn’t move.

He glanced up. “Unless you want to boost me. I warn you, I’m a little heavier than you are.”

“I’ll go.” She stepped into his hands and raised her arms over her head.

Montana straightened, lifting her up as he did.

She found a loose panel in the ceiling, pushed it upward and then poked her head through. "I can see the fourth floor landing. We should be able to get out through here."

"I'm going to raise you high enough to get your arms through, and you can take it from there."

Montana lifted her until Kate got her arms through the hole, braced her elbows on the sides and pulled herself up to sit on the edge. Once she had her breath, she pushed to her feet and shone the light back into the elevator car. "Your turn. Need me to lend you a hand?"

"No, thanks." He jumped, his fingers catching on the sides of the panel opening.

Kate backed up as much as possible, directing the flashlight beam near Montana without blinding him. He pulled himself up, his biceps flexing, stretching the shirt tight around his chest and shoulders. Squeezing his shoulders through the tight space, he soon had the rest of his body through and stood beside Kate.

She handed him the light and stepped over to the fourth floor landing and down onto the hallway floor.

Emergency lighting glowed softly, giving just enough light to guide them.

"Follow me." Montana led the way, turning left at the end of the corridor. Midway down the next hall, he pushed through a doorway. "Everyone okay in here?" he called out.

A strong flashlight beam shone in his face. Montana raised an arm to shade his eyes.

"Montana, is that you?" a voice called out.

Kate entered the room behind the Navy SEAL to find it crowded with guys as big and brawny as Montana, crowded around a couple of battery-operated lanterns. Interspersed with the big men were a few women and a white-haired man who appeared to be as physically fit as the younger men.

"Anyone sustain injuries?" Montana asked.

"We're all good here. Thankfully, we were in the war room when the explosion occurred," the white-haired man said. "I'm glad we put the extra money in the construction. It's built like a bunker." He stepped forward. "I'm betting this is our chameleon, Kate McKenzie. Hi, I'm Royce Fontaine, the head of Stealth Operations Specialists—or SOS, as we like to refer to it."

"SOS?" Kate raised her brows. "Just what does SOS do?"

Royce nodded, a smile tipping the corners of his mouth. "Stealth Operations Specialists is a team of agents called in when the FBI,

CIA and Secret Service can't quite get the job done. Or the situation is highly sensitive and needs the utmost secrecy. Unfortunately, most of my agents are assigned at this time, thus the need to call in reinforcements." He swept his arm out, his gaze circling the room. "Glad to have you all on board for this operation. We can use all the help we can get."

Kate nodded, her gaze seeking and finding her old roommate from college, Becca Smith. "I didn't realize there'd be an entire team of people on this gig."

Becca pushed through the others and hugged Kate. "I couldn't say much over the phone. We needed you here, where others can't listen in on the conversation. As we've learned the hard way, we can't trust anyone but the people in this room."

"And based on the explosion outside the building," Royce said, "there are those who will stop at nothing to keep us from doing our jobs. Don't worry. I have people checking the structure. They will alert us if we need to evacuate immediately. When we had the structure built, we hardened it for just such an occasion. We could potentially continue to work out of this office, but coming and going from a targeted location will be dangerous."

Kate leaned toward Becca and whispered,

"What are you getting me into?" Her body quivered with excitement. She'd trained for covert ops. This was what made her blood sing.

Becca took her hand. "Come into the conference room. Geek is working on getting the computers and lighting back online so we can brief you. Then I'm sure we'll move to our backup location. This building has been compromised."

As Becca led her through another door, Kate glanced over her shoulder, searching for and finding Montana. Though she'd met him only a few minutes before, he seemed to be the anchor in this sea of people, with their plans that threatened to sweep her away from a desk job she loathed.

Becca had promised her a way to redeem and reclaim her status in the CIA, if they could pull off this mission. By the looks of it, and the people squeezing into the war room, they could well be a small army gathering to overthrow the government, for all Kate knew.

What had she gotten herself into?

Whatever it was, it sure beat the hell out of pushing paper.

Chapter Two

Montana followed everyone into the conference room, amazed they weren't evacuating, despite Fontaine's assurance that the building could withstand a bomb blast.

Several flashlights and a couple of lanterns provided enough illumination that he could get around without tripping on the many people crowded into the large room.

"Take a seat," Fontaine commanded. "The lights should come on momentar—"

The fluorescent bulbs blinked overhead and then glowed brightly.

A collective sigh and smiles were shared all around. Montana pulled out a chair for Kate and waited while she sank into it. Then he sat beside her. Now that everyone was in and seated around the large table, he had a chance to study the people Fontaine had gathered.

"I want to start by introducing everyone,"

Fontaine said. "You're all to be part of the team in one fashion or another." He pointed to the man who entered carrying a laptop. "The heart of this group is Geek, our computer guru and all-around technical genius." The white-haired man waved his hand toward the man helping Geek with wires and switches. "Lance will be working with him in the office or in a communication van, wherever we need him to support the operation."

Fontaine waved next at a woman Montana knew from their failed attempt to vacation in Cancun, Becca Smith, who worked directly for Fontaine as one of his SOS agents. "Becca Smith has a stake in this operation. Whoever is behind all the assassinations and attempts killed her father and tried to kill her father's close friend, Oscar Melton. Both of them were top-notch CIA agents working with the congressional Subcommittee on Terrorism, Drug Trafficking and International Operations."

Turning to his left, Fontaine held his hand out to a nice-looking woman with blond hair and blue eyes. She, too, had been involved in the chaos of Cancun. "Natalie Layne is another SOS agent who has been a part of the ongoing issues we've encountered thus far. Her sister was one of the women abducted, with the intent to sell her in a human trafficking ring located out of Cancun, Mexico."

Fontaine continued around the table. "Besides the SOS operatives, please welcome Kate McKenzie, an agent with the CIA. We've also been augmented by six Navy SEALs, on loan to us from Stennis, Mississippi."

Starting around the room, Fontaine introduced them. "Dutton Callaway, who goes by Duff. Sawyer Houston, Quentin Lovett, Jace Hunter, Cord Schafer, who goes by Rip, and Benjamin Raines, nicknamed after his home state of Montana."

Montana nodded acknowledgment.

"A six pack of SEALs," Geek muttered, as he connected the laptop to an Ethernet cable and clicked a remote that lit a projection screen at one end of the long room.

"Are we planning to start a war with all of these people in the room?" Duff, one of Montana's SEAL teammates, asked.

Fontaine shook his head, his jaw tightening. "No, but by the looks of it, we might be stopping one that's been going on longer than we knew." He turned to Geek. "Ready?"

Geek nodded. "Someone get the door."

Navy SEAL Quentin Lovett, standing near the back of the room, shut the door.

At the same time, Geek clicked a handheld remote control device and the image on his laptop projected onto the screen. He touched the keyboard and the screen filled with a lot of what appeared to be random numbers.

"This is what we have so far," Fontaine said. "Thanks to Becca's father, God rest his soul, who knew he was in trouble and might not live to tell about it."

"All I see are numbers," Montana pointed out. "Do they represent something?"

"Geek has spent the past week crunching these numbers, trying to decode them, thinking they were a special message." Fontaine nodded toward him. "Tell them what you discovered."

"Well, I couldn't make secret messages out of them, and I was getting really frustrated, until I took a step back and just stared at the groupings. Then it hit me." He stood and pointed to the wall. "This half of each sixteen-digit number is a date." He pointed to the other half. "The other eight digits could have been bank accounts, safe-deposit box numbers or anything else in the world. Given that they were all eight digits in length, I made a calculated guess and ran a program, entering them as coordinates."

He walked back to the computer and clicked

another key. A world map replaced the numbers. Bright red dots overlaid the map.

Montana leaned forward, his eyes narrowed, and studied the information depicted on the image.

Geek zoomed in on the map, focusing on Europe. He walked toward the screen again. "On the date for this location, in Paris, France, a terrorist attack took place, killing everyone in a certain restaurant, including Harmon Whitlow, his wife, son and daughter-in-law."

"I heard about that," Sawyer said. One of the six SEALs at the table, he knew the most about politics. As the son of a former US Senator, he kept up with the political scene, though he claimed he couldn't care less.

He always amazed Montana with his insight on what was going on in Washington, DC.

After the fiasco in Cancun, where someone had attempted to kill him and his father, Sawyer had been a little less adamant about his distaste for politics. With his father now in the equivalent of the witness protection program, starting a new life as someone else, Sawyer had volunteered for this mission, determined to find the person or persons responsible for trying to kill them. "Harmon Whitlow was the undersecretary for political affairs in the US State Department," he stated.

Geek nodded and pointed to another dot, this time on the map of the US. "On this date in New York City, a bomb went off near a set of bleachers during the NYC Marathon. Two people died in that attack, over two hundred people were injured and one went missing."

"Who?" Kate asked.

"Emily Brantley, daughter of Trevor Brantley, multimillionaire." Geek pressed a key on the laptop, displaying a photo of a pretty young lady standing between a man in a suit and a well-dressed woman. "She was running the marathon. When the smoke cleared, she was gone. Her bodyguards had been killed not by the bomb, but by bullets that expertly pierced their skulls."

Montana knew about Brantley's missing daughter. It had been all over the news, with pleas and a reward posted from the Brantleys for their daughter's safe return.

Fontaine interjected, "The authorities assumed it was a terrorist bombing by members of ISIS, a copycat of the 2013 attack at the Boston Marathon. *We* think it was a diversion allowing the bombers to kill the bodyguards and nab the Brantley woman."

"How soon after the bombing was Trevor Brantley murdered?" Montana asked.

Geek pointed to a larger dot on the map in the vicinity of Washington, DC. "On this date, at this coordinate, less than two weeks later, Trevor Brantley was gunned down in his mansion here."

Sawyer pointed at the double dots on the Yucatan Peninsula. "Were those the dates and locations of the attempts on my life and my father's?"

Geek nodded. "Yes. Obviously those attempts weren't successful."

Becca Smith, her face pale, asked, "Was one of those dots on the nation's capital the day my father was killed near his apartment here? Is that why there are more dots in the DC area? Multiple killings?"

Geek's lips twisted. "The date your father died and the date there was an attempt on his colleague Oscar Melton's life were both on that list, with the coordinates of the attacks."

Montana's teammate Quentin Lovett slipped an arm around Becca's waist. "We know the connection between Marcus Smith and Oscar Melton. What connection is there between them and all the others?"

"Besides investigating the drug and human trafficking issues worldwide, the two CIA agents were investigating these codes. I can only assume they thought they were connected. Marcus Smith was able to mail the disk containing the information to Becca before he was killed. Oscar Melton is still in critical condition in a coma."

"We suspect Sawyer's father, Rand Houston, was targeted because he was on the Subcommittee for Terrorism, Drug Trafficking and International Operations," Fontaine said. "What we can't connect is Trevor Brantley and his family to the others. Which leads me to one more introduction, for those who haven't had the pleasure of meeting her." He turned toward the door, smiled and held out his hand. "Perfect timing. Please, come in."

A woman with long dark hair, wearing a tailored gray skirt suit, stepped into the room. Montana remembered her from their operation to rescue women in Cancun. She'd come undercover as a potential buyer. Montana recognized the man following her as Rex, her bodyguard.

Fontaine took the woman's hand. "This is Mica Brantley, Trevor Brantley's widow. Since her husband's death, she's made it her mission to find and bring her stepdaughter, Emily Brantley, home."

Mica nodded at the roomful of people.

"Thank you for volunteering for this mission. I won't rest until Emily is home safe and my husband's killer is brought to justice."

"Mrs. Brantley was not in the country on the date her husband was murdered in their home," Fontaine said. "She's had multiple attempts made on her life but managed to get here despite her pursuers."

Mica nodded. "Since Trevor's death, I've lived aboard my yacht and traveled, searching for Emily. I'll never give up hope of finding her. I love the girl as if she were my own."

Fontaine nodded. "She's taken a huge risk to come back to DC, offering herself as bait to catch the killer."

Mica gave a brief, sad smile. "I've spent a lot of money and time searching and thus far haven't found the source of all the tragedy. Royce has been in contact with me since the incident in Cancun. When he learned about the disk, he thought I should know." She lifted her chin. "I'm tired of running. If I can put myself up as the target, maybe we can flush out the killer, or catch one of his hit men and interrogate him."

"That's a dangerous proposition," Kate said. "You're willing to risk your life for this effort?"

"I am." Mica turned to Fontaine. "With the

understanding that, should I die in this attempt, someone continue to look for Emily."

Fontaine nodded. "We'll do our best to keep you alive and find Emily." He glanced around, making eye contact with everyone in the room. "We're all in this together. We have to stop those behind all the murders and attempted murders in this case."

As one, everyone in the room nodded.

Montana's sense of justice refused to let him back down from this mission. He'd seen the women held captive for auction. No woman, or her family, should be subjected to the horror of human trafficking. He wanted to get to the bottom of the case as much as Mica Brantley did.

Montana tipped his head toward the screen, ready to get on with solving the case. "What about the rest of the dates and coordinates?"

"We connected the dots with a couple of 'accidents,'" Geek said. "Richard Giddings drove off a bridge into the Potomac. He worked with Senator Houston on the same subcommittee. Percy Beardon, an avid cyclist, fell from his bike at this coordinate on the date indicated."

"What's the deal on Beardon?" Duff asked.

Fontaine shook his head. "His claim to fame was that he was one of the survivors of the Syrian attack on the US Embassy in Turkey a couple of years ago."

"Most of the dates are past," Sawyer said.

"Like notches on a bedpost?" Quentin asked.

Montana's lips twitched. Trust Quentin to make it about sex. The man was an expert ladies' man and charmer. At least until he'd met his match. Becca had been good for him. She made him work to woo her. And now that they were in a committed relationship, they were seldom apart.

Montana was glad for his friend. Quentin had needed someone to come home to. He'd settled down and quit going out as much. Too bad they worked so far apart, with Becca based out of Virginia and Quentin out of Mississippi. But then Fontaine didn't care where his SOS operatives lived, as long as they could deploy at a moment's notice. Montana suspected Becca would soon base out of Mississippi, to be closer to Quentin when she wasn't working an assignment.

Familiar with those conditions, Montana didn't envy Quentin and Becca's relationship. As often as SBT-22 was deployed, and given the nature of Becca's work, the two would be hard-pressed to get together on a regular basis, even if she was based out of Mississippi.

Montana had always considered that as long as he was on active duty as a Navy SEAL, he'd be better off steering clear of entanglements. Being a bachelor was the safest bet.

He glanced at his new partner, Kate McKenzie. The woman seemed no-nonsense and decidedly kick-ass. He shouldn't have a problem sticking to his intent to stay single and emotionally unavailable to women. Especially one who'd tackled him before they'd been properly introduced.

Those steely eyes didn't inspire him to lose himself in her. Her athletic body and shoulder-length, straight, sandy-blond hair didn't make him want to run his hand through it to ascertain just how silky the strands were.

Well, maybe just a little. And her eyes were a startling steel-gray, rimmed with a darker pewter outline.

When she'd lain on top of him, protecting him from potential shrapnel, he hadn't been all that turned on by the rounded swells of her breasts against his chest.

Okay, so maybe he had noticed her breasts. They had been smashed against him for what had felt like an eternity. When he'd rested his hands on her hips, his body had naturally reacted to having a female on top of him. A lot of time had passed since he'd been with a woman.

He turned to study his new partner and frowned. It was so much easier to work with men. They didn't threaten his determination to remain footloose and single.

Dragging his attention from Kate, he focused on Fontaine. "Most of the dates are past. That means some of them are in the future. Like a schedule of events to come. You agree with that, don't you?"

Geek and Fontaine nodded simultaneously.

"That's exactly what we've learned," Fontaine said.

"So how do we fit in with this mission?" Kate asked. "Why did you need me when you had all of these people to run your operation?"

Fontaine faced Montana and Kate. "Becca tells me you are an expert chameleon, able to change your appearance to look like anyone you want."

Kate shrugged. "I did a lot of theater in high school and college. My skills with makeup came in handy as a field agent with CIA. I had a knack for transforming into whomever I needed to be." Her lips thinned and her jaw tightened.

Montana noted this little change in her

expression. That she spoke in the past tense made him curious. Wasn't she still an agent in the CIA?

Fontaine nodded and his gaze shifted to Montana. "Raines, your team considers you the best at camouflage and bombs."

Montana frowned. "Sure. I can blend in with any tree, bush or desert location. But nothing like Kate."

"Your abilities to blend in were only part of the reason I chose you two for this assignment." Fontaine waved his hand. "If you could please stand, I'll show you the other reason."

Montana stood and held Kate's chair while she rose as well, her brows pulling together.

"Mrs. Brantley, I'd like you and your bodyguard to please stand by Raines and McKenzie."

The two complied.

Fontaine smiled. "Perfect. Kate, you're almost the exact height as Mrs. Brantley. And Raines, you're pretty close to Rex Masters's height and build."

"So?" Montana challenged.

Geek pointed to a dot on the map. "One of the dates indicates tomorrow at the yacht club."

Fontaine picked up from there. "Mrs. Brantley is listed as keynote speaker at the annual fund-raiser the club sponsors for the children's hospital."

"I've canceled every other engagement I've had since my husband's death," Mica said. "This was one I couldn't. The children's hospital is near and dear to my heart. After losing my baby to leukemia, I realized how much the hospital does for desperately ill children and their families. I'll be there."

"Based on the date and coordinates, someone knows you wouldn't miss the event," Fontaine said. "We can't be certain just who will be targeted, but we wanted to make sure you're safe. Raines and McKenzie will go as your guests. We created identities for them as newly rich recent members of the yacht club."

"Are we to supplement Mrs. Brantley's bodyguard support?" Kate asked.

"Yes, and more," Fontaine said. "I'll have several of the other SEALs and some of my agents augmenting the waitstaff at the club."

Geek added, "We can't be certain who they will target. Because whoever is orchestrating these attacks doesn't seem to be going after just the politicians and federal agents..." He paused. "They're taking out the family members, too."

Mrs. Brantley's face paled. "Perhaps I should

call and cancel my speech at the fund-raiser. I'd hate for a bomb, targeting me, to take out innocent bystanders."

"That's why we'll have the SEALs and SOS team in place," Fontaine assured her. "I'll also have bomb-sniffing dogs make a thorough sweep of the entire building before the event commences, and we'll have security cordon off the area to keep vehicles from getting close."

Mrs. Brantley chewed on her bottom lip. "I don't want people hurt because of me."

"We don't know who they will be after," Geek said. "And as far as we can tell, nobody knows we have the list of dates and coordinates."

Fontaine turned to Montana. "Raines, you and McKenzie will be there not only to protect Mrs. Brantley, you are to watch and listen closely to the people she interacts with. If we determine she is a target, you two might have to take Mrs. Brantley's and Masters's places in the DC scene as their doubles for a while."

Montana exchanged glances with Rex Masters. It made sense that he would replace the man. They were similar in build and he could have his hair lightened to match Masters's dark blond cropped hair. Kate and Mica were the same height and close to the same build.

Mrs. Brantley might have a tinier waist and bigger breasts, but Kate, if she was as good as she said she was, could make her face up to look just like Mica's. Colored contacts would help match Mica's dark brown irises.

"Why aren't you using your SOS agents instead of the SEALs?" asked Navy SEAL Jace Hunter, the youngest member of the SBT-22 team.

"I'm short staffed," Fontaine said. "They're on critical missions throughout the country and the world. Considering the successful kill rate of that list, we might need all the security and waitstaff we can get. The future dates and locations are in or around the DC area at major events. Geek and I conducted a thorough background check on the six of you SEALs. You all have exemplary records. I'd trust you with my life and that of Mrs. Brantley. Add to it the fact that most of you have already been involved in the attacks, and I think you have a stake in seeing it to a satisfactory conclusion."

"We usually work in combat environments," Duff said. "Mingling with the rich and famous might be a bit out of our league."

"Again," Fontaine said, "I don't know who else I could trust. When we took down the assassin after Oscar Melton, we found a mole in the CIA orchestrating some of the assassinations. We don't know how deep into our nation's security the problem exists."

Montana's fists clenched. They were all supposed to be on the same side. When the organization had bad seeds within it, people lost faith, and the infrastructure of that entity crumbled from within. After all they'd been through in Cancun, and the multiple attempts on his friend Sawyer's life, he would be happy to see this operation to the bitter end. "I'm in."

"WHY ME?" KATE faced Royce. "I'm with the CIA. As far as you know, I could be as rotten as the deputy director you brought down."

Her friend Becca stepped forward. "I vouched for you. My father and Oscar only had good things to say about your work and your integrity. They trusted you."

Kate's cheeks heated. "Even after my demotion?"

Becca nodded. "Especially after. You couldn't know your partner was a double agent. I'm betting you learned a valuable lesson from the whole affair."

Out of the corner of her eye, Kate saw Montana's face jerk toward her.

Well, to hell with him. People made mistakes. Unfortunately, she'd made a double-whammy mistake. Falling for her partner was bad enough. Not doing her homework to learn the man she was sleeping with was actually a Russian double agent was worse. Kate was lucky she hadn't been kicked out of the CIA. Being demoted from field agent to desk duty had been bad, but not the end of her career.

With a sigh, she pushed the past behind her and glanced at Mica. "I'll need to get inside your head and know your moves, expressions, likes and dislikes, as well as who your friends are, and known enemies."

Mica smiled. "I like the way you think." Her smile faded. "But if I *am* a target, and you take my place, you'll become the target." She shook her head and turned to Royce. "I can't put Kate in that position."

"If it helps uncover who's after you, I'm in," Kate said. "Hell, if it gets me out of desk duty, I'll do just about anything."

Royce glanced at Montana. "What about you, Raines? Are you up for playing dress-up and body-double?"

Montana shrugged. "As I said, I'm in."

Mica Brantley nodded. "Thank you both. I hope nothing bad comes of the yacht club fund-raiser. It's supposed to be all about the children and raising money for them."

"Our aim is to make certain nothing happens," Royce assured her.

"Then I'll see you all at the event." Mica stared around the room. "In some form or fashion. Thank you for your assistance in this matter. I was running out of alternatives. I'm hoping with your help to recover my stepdaughter."

"We're looking into that. Geek and Lance have been searching the internet and backtracking through all the footage of the marathon."

Mica's eyes widened. "Anything new?"

Royce shook his head. "Nothing yet, but we're not done."

Her shoulders slumped. "Thank you for all you've done thus far."

With a dip of his head, Royce squeezed her hand. "Until tomorrow."

After Mica left the room with Rex, Royce returned his attention to the group. "Any questions?"

Her mind already ten steps ahead, Kate raked her gaze over Montana. "We'll need clothes and shoes."

"I have clothes and shoes," Montana said.

Royce grinned. "Trust Kate. You'll need new clothes and shoes. And they won't be cheap. Don't worry about budget or what to buy. I have one of my agents on standby at a local high-end clothier. She'll guide you two on selections and then arrange for your makeover."

Montana's brows dipped, and the SEALs around the table chuckled.

"Going preppy on us, Montana?" the man Royce had introduced as Jace Hunter asked.

"Don't go hookin' up with some rich hoochie mama," the one nicknamed Rip said. "Your country needs you as a SEAL, not a bonbon-eating gigolo."

Rip's comment had all the guys laughing.

Kate got a strange amount of enjoyment from Montana's discomfort. At the same time, she couldn't wait to see the big man decked out in a suit and tie. Then again…if she thought he was ruggedly handsome in jeans, with a T-shirt stretching tautly over his massive chest…she might have palpitations over this SEAL's magnetism in a suit or tuxedo.

Get a grip.

Kate squared her shoulders. "When do we start?"

"There's a company car pulling up to the back of the building now." Royce turned to the others in the room. "We could use some help clearing the building and moving to our disaster recovery site."

Everyone rose at once, talking and moving toward the door.

Kate went through first.

Becca caught up with her. "I'll show you the way out the back."

Once Montana joined them, they headed along the hallway, dimly lit by emergency lighting. Becca opened a door to a stairwell and they descended to the ground level.

When Becca reached for the exit door, Montana covered her hand with his. "Let me go first."

Becca snorted. "At this point, we're all tactical. Male or female, we're trained in urban warfare."

"You and Kate might be trained in urban warfare, but I've *survived* urban warfare. And if that's not good enough, my mama taught me to open doors for ladies." He winked and stepped around her.

Kate's heart skipped several beats at the sexy wink.

Becca turned to her friend with a smile. "Oh, he's *smooth*, that one."

Montana exited the building, closing the door behind him. A moment later, he opened it and held it for the women.

Becca stood back. “I’m not actually going with you. I need to help move operations to the backup location.”

Kate hugged her. “Thanks for thinking of me.”

Her friend squeezed her tightly. “I figured you were perfect for this job. Stay safe.”

“I will.” Kate released Becca.

Montana stood beside a long, black, chauffeur-driven car, holding the door for her.

Kate gave him a crooked grin.

“I told you,” he said. “My mama taught me to treat the ladies right.”

“Your mother would be proud,” she said, and slid into the backseat, scooting over far enough to allow room for Montana.

So this was it. The start of a potentially dangerous operation, with a hunk of a SEAL as her sidekick, and a chance to redeem herself if things turned out okay. She couldn’t help but cross her fingers and pray this mission went off like clockwork, they nailed the persons responsible for the hits and brought the Brantley girl home alive.

Chapter Three

Montana hated shopping. After trying on the fourth set of trousers, the fifth button-down shirt and the third suit jacket, he'd had enough. "What's wrong with this one?" he asked. Other than he'd probably rip the damned thing when he went after the bad guys. One right uppercut and he'd bust out the stitches.

SOS Agent Nicole Steele, who preferred to go by her nickname of Tazer, shook her head. "We need to go another size larger. You can't move in that jacket. Good Lord, Ben, what do they feed men in Montana?" She waved to the attendant and asked him to bring another size larger. "We have a seamstress on standby to make the alterations quickly."

"Seriously, I don't need but one suit and a pair of casual pants."

"Not if you want to blend in with the rich

and politically elevated," Tazer said. "Now quit bellyaching. How did you ever make it through BUD/S training?"

"I sure as hell didn't have to wear a suit and dress shirt. I only had to worry about drowning in the sea or falling flat on my face in the mud. For that matter, it was a cakewalk compared to this."

"Big baby. You'll be happy when it fits properly," Tazer said. "Hurry up. We still have to get Kate tricked out."

Kate sat beside Tazer, her lips twitching.

Montana pointed a finger. "Don't say a word."

She held up her hands. "Did I?"

"No, but I can feel you want to."

She drew a line across her lips. "My lips are sealed." Her gray eyes flashed. "But if I were to say something, it would be along the lines of 'think of these clothes as a uniform.'"

"Not helping," he said, and yanked the jacket off his shoulders.

The attendant handed him another jacket and quickly stepped back, as if afraid Montana would take a swing at him.

Montana shrugged into the garment. The sooner he got through this, the better. He knew what size jeans he wore and the brand that fit best. When he needed a new pair, he walked into the store, picked them out of the stacks and headed straight for the checkout counter. The end.

As the jacket settled around his shoulders, Montana hated to admit Tazer was right. This one wasn't nearly as constricting and actually felt good on his body.

"Much better. Now, button the jacket." Tazer and the attendant converged on him. While Tazer tugged, the clerk pinned. When they were done, Montana was afraid to move for fear of being stuck by one of the hundreds of pins sticking out of the material. He felt like a cross between a voodoo doll and a dressmaker's dummy.

Then they went to work on the trousers, tugging and tucking the hem and the waistband. When they were done, Montana was hot, cranky and ready to be out of the building.

"Let me have the jacket." Tazer held out her hands.

Montana started to take it off and was jabbed by a pin. "Ouch!"

"Here, let me." Kate stood, eased the jacket from his shoulders and handed it to Tazer.

Tazer handed the jacket to the attendant, who hustled out of the room, presumably to take the garment to the seamstress.

"Now, out of those trousers." Tazer held out her hands again.

Kate backed away. "Sorry. Can't help you there."

"Hurry up." Tazer snapped her fingers. "We don't have all day. Trust me, you don't have anything I haven't seen before."

Montana glared. "You haven't seen *my* anything before."

Kate's lips stretched into a wide grin and she turned her back, chuckling.

Montana stripped out of the trousers and slipped into his jeans.

"I'll be back shortly with the clothes you'll wear out of here." Tazer left the dressing area.

Montana buttoned his jeans. "You can turn around now."

Kate faced him. "I would have thought a SEAL would have no trouble stripping in front of a woman."

"My mama—"

Kate waved her hand. "Yeah, yeah. Your mama taught you better. But you're a SEAL. You fight hard and play rough."

He shrugged. "It's just who I am. I was taught to respect women, no matter how young or old."

Kate shook her head. "You can take the

cowboy out of Montana, but you can't take the Montana out of the cowboy?"

"Something like that." He tipped his head toward her. "What about you? Where did you grow up?"

She shook her head. "I was a military brat. We moved fifteen times before I turned eighteen. I'm not *from* anywhere."

"What about your folks? Did your father retire somewhere you call home?" he asked.

Kate nodded. "He passed away. My mother has a condo in Wisconsin and she now works for a pediatrician."

"I take it you don't see her often." Montana sat in one of the chairs and shoved his foot into one of his cowboy boots.

She stared in the direction Tazer had gone. "Not often enough. What about you?"

"I haven't been back to Montana in two years. Just never seems to be enough time."

"Where in Montana?" Kate turned toward him, her gaze capturing his.

"On a ranch south of Bozeman."

"So you're the real deal, then."

"If you mean I'm a real cowboy, then yes. I've done just about everything that needs doing on a cattle ranch." He pulled the second boot on and stood. "Enough about me.

What about you? Why did they demote you in the CIA?"

She turned away, her mouth thinning into a firm line. "I'd rather not talk about it."

"Suit yourself. But the more we know about each other, the better we will be able to work together. If I didn't know my buddies on my SEAL team as well as I do, I wouldn't be able to anticipate their reactions to different situations."

"Fine." She faced him, a frown pulling her brows together. "I screwed up. I fell for my partner, and he just happened to be a double agent for Russia." She sighed. "I was a green rookie. I thought everyone who signed on with the CIA had been fully vetted and loved our country as much as I do." Kate lifted her chin and stared straight into Montana's eyes. "I learned my lesson. Don't put your full faith and trust in anyone. And don't fall for your partner."

Montana nodded. "I'm sorry that happened to you. Must have hurt pretty bad." He stepped toward the door. "You don't have to worry about this partner. I'm a confirmed bachelor, and I've never even been to Russia." He winked at her. "Let's go find Tazer. It's your turn to play dress-up."

Montana had asked the hard question, but

he'd rather know who he was working with and what made her tick. When the crap hit the fan, he wanted to know what she was made of and how she would react.

Kate McKenzie had taken a hit. More than likely, she wouldn't trust him easily. He'd have to ease into her confidence a little at a time. He sure as hell hoped they had time to make that happen. In a life-and-death situation, Kate needed to know he had her six. He already knew she had his, based on the flying tackle she'd initiated earlier.

While the seamstress worked on the suit jacket and trousers for Montana, Tazer led them to the exclusive shop next door. Where the men's shop was all dark wood and masculine, this one was light and airy. What amazed him was the lack of clothes racks.

"Are they hiding the ladies' clothing?" he whispered into Kate's ear.

She glanced around. "No idea. Normally, I can't afford to walk into a shop like this. Royce must have one helluva budget."

The beautifully dressed and tastefully made-up attendant in high heels and perfect accessories shot a glance at Kate and Montana and then turned her attention to Tazer. "How might I help you?"

If the woman had thought to have an attitude about finding clothing for Kate, Tazer set her in her place quickly.

Tazer took Montana's arm, pointed to a cushioned seat and ordered, "Sit."

The attendant took Kate to a dressing room and then disappeared into the back of the shop with Tazer. They returned with a handful of dresses, blouses and trousers, and disappeared into the dressing room.

Already antsy and ready to be outside, Montana rose from the cushioned seat and paced.

Tazer emerged from the dressing room, looked around and spotted Montana. She pointed a finger. "You. Come with me."

She took him to the back of the salon, where a barber's chair stood in the middle of a small office. A woman with bright blue hair, armed with scissors and a comb, smiled at him. "Let's get started."

Unsure as to what they were to "get started" on, Montana shot a glance at Tazer.

She hooked his arm, led him to the chair and pointed. "Sit."

Montana's brows rose. "I'm beginning to feel like a dog in training."

"Then act like one, and do as instructed." Tazer clapped her hands sharply. "Come on, we don't have all day. You two have a meeting tonight."

"We do?"

"Yes. I'll fill you in once we're through the transformation."

Half bent toward the seat, Montana paused. "Transformation?"

Tazer rolled her eyes. "Trust me."

He figured hair grew back, but his buddies wouldn't let him live down blue hair. Still, he knew they didn't have time to argue, and Tazer seemed to know what she was doing.

Montana sat.

"By the way, I'm Karen," said the hairstylist. "This shouldn't take too long."

Her scissors flashed and hair flew around him. She shaved his face with a wicked-looking straight razor, trimmed his eyebrows and plucked some of the wild hairs.

So far, he didn't have a problem with what she'd done. He'd needed a haircut after being on vacation for two weeks, and his brows were a little on the bushy side. But when she brought out a bowl with powder and mixed in liquid from a bottle, he held up his hand. "What's that?"

"Bleach."

"For what?" he asked, leaning away from

the bowl and what appeared to be a wide, flat paintbrush she was using to stir the contents.

"I'm going to lighten your hair." She held up a photo of Rex Masters, Mica's bodyguard. "I'm told you need to have this hair color."

"Yeah, but will it be permanent?"

She shook her head. "It'll grow out in a couple months."

"Months!"

"Relax. It's just hair. With your tan, the blond will look fabulous on you."

Not liking the gleam in Karen's eyes, Montana sat back and allowed the stylist to do her job. Tazer chose that hour to be absent.

Figures.

By the time the stylist finished and dried his hair, Montana was ready to bust through whatever doors stood in his way to getting outside.

Karen slapped a handheld mirror in his palm. "See? You look great."

He glanced into the mirror, relieved he didn't have blue hair, and was amazed at the resemblance between him and Mica Brantley's bodyguard.

Karen had even lightened his eyebrows to a shade darker than his now sandy-blond hair.

"Good, you're done." Tazer appeared in

the doorway with an armful of clothes. "Put these on."

"Ever consider the word *please*?" Montana asked. The SOS agent might dress like a fashion model, but she was as lacking in manners as some of his SEAL buddies.

"No time." Again, she clapped her hands. "Chop, chop!" Tazer disappeared again, leaving Montana with the stylist, who was gathering the tools of her trade.

"Thank you, Karen." Montana pulled his wallet out of his pocket, prepared to tip the woman for a job well done.

She held up her hand. "No need to tip me. Miss Steele took care of everything. It was a pleasure." She held out a card. "Look me up if you're ever at a loose end." With a wink, she left the office, closing the door behind her.

Montana shucked his clothes and slipped into the trousers and matching suit jacket, freshly altered. Though he preferred jeans and T-shirts, he had to admit the outfit, now that it had been adjusted, fit like a second skin. He drew the line at putting on the silk tie. Dressed, buttoned and wearing the new patent leather shoes Tazer had delivered with the suit, he stepped out of the office and went in search of Tazer and Kate.

The female attendant he'd met earlier found

him wandering through the warehouse of dresses and clothes, and took his arm. "Miss Steele asked that you wait in the viewing area until the ladies are ready." She ushered him into the lounge with the dressing room doors Kate had disappeared behind earlier.

Montana paced, his patience worn thin, his need to get outside an obsession.

Fifteen very long minutes later, Tazer walked out of the back warehouse area.

Kate followed, wearing a pale cream skirt suit that fit her long, athletic body like a kid glove. The matching high heels made her legs look even longer, the tight muscles of her calves bunching with each step.

Montana's groin tightened and he fought to keep his jaw from dropping to the floor.

Her shoulder-length hair had been swept back into one of those French twist things women liked to wear. She looked amazing.

Kate's gaze swept him from top to bottom. "I like you with dark hair better," she said. "But you'll do."

"Not to worry." Tazer nodded to the attendant. "Could you get the handbag I left in the back?"

She nodded and hurried through the door.

Once they were alone, Tazer handed Montana a bottle of dark liquid. "Before you go out tonight, put this in your hair and let it dry. You two are now Monty and Kayla Lindemann, good friends of the Brantleys. While you're Monty, you'll put the dye in your hair. When you have to switch to fill in for Rex, just wash it out."

"What about me?" Kate asked. "I can't just dye my hair black in a flash."

"No, but you can wear this." She handed Kate a bag.

Kate fished inside and pulled a wig halfway out. It was long, dark and straight, like Mica Brantley's hair. Kate nodded. "Got it."

"I've arranged for you and Mica to have matching outfits for the yacht club gala. You will arrive as the Lindemanns, but if anything happens that puts Mrs. Brantley in danger, we're pulling her and Rex out and putting you two in as their replacements."

"The event is tomorrow. What's happening tonight?" Montana asked.

"You're going to meet up with Mica at the Jefferson Hotel in downtown DC. She has the Martha Jefferson Penthouse Suite. The Lindemanns will be a floor below. You're having dinner together. We'll have the hotel covered with your SEAL team and SOS electronic surveillance." She handed Montana a leather briefcase. "Everything you'll need is in the case. Familiarize yourselves with the contents on the way over. Once inside the hotel, consider everything bugged. Act, live, breathe as if you really are the Lindemanns. We don't know how deep the traitors are entrenched and in what government entities. Trust no one but the members of the team."

Montana nodded, his free hand tightening into a fist. To think there were traitors within the organizations he would have thought he could trust made him all the more determined to take them down.

KATE AND MONTANA stepped through the front door of the dress shop and slid into the waiting limousine. Their new clothes had been packed into designer luggage and stored in the trunk of the car. They would take the long way around the city, be dropped off at the airport and later picked up by Mica Brantley's car.

Montana opened the case Tazer had given him and extracted their orders and a dossier detailing who they were supposed to be, how they'd met Mica and her husband and why they were visiting her at the Jefferson.

"Mica and Trevor introduced us to each other in Paris." Kate turned to Montana. "Have you been to Paris?"

His lips twisted. "I might prefer Montana to the big cities, but yes, I've been to Paris. How about you?"

She nodded. Her partner had taken her to Paris over a long weekend between assignments. Little had she known he had used their weekend away as an opportunity to pass information to his Russian contact. God, she'd been a fool, thinking he was in love with her and out getting little French pastries for their breakfasts. All along, he'd been working.

"Hey." Montana touched a finger to her chin. "We're supposed to be newlyweds. No long faces."

"Sorry." She read through the pages, committing the words to memory. "I've got this. Do you need to see it again?"

"No."

"It says to shred the documents." Kate glanced around the inside of the limousine. It didn't surprise her to find a shredder. One last glance at the pages and she pushed them through the device.

Montana extracted a ring box from the case and opened it. "Hold out your left hand."

Kate did as he asked.

"With this ring, I thee fake wed. I promise to have your six and pretend to love, honor and cherish you until this op is over." Montana slipped on the engagement ring with the huge emerald cut diamond and matching wedding band.

Kate snorted. "Cute." His big hands felt rough against hers, but warm and strong. She could imagine them sliding across her bare skin. With a start, she yanked her hand away. Now was not the time to be daydreaming about the man who would play her husband. "God, I hope this isn't real. It looks like at least three carats."

He removed the larger, plain wedding band from the box and started to slip it onto his ring finger.

"Wait." Kate took the band from him. "It's only fair."

Montana's lips quirked. "I've never been accused of being unfair."

"Well, don't start now," she said. "With this ring, I thee fake wed. I promise to save your butt, should the need arise...*again*. And should you try anything without my permission, I promise to hurt you." Kate raised her brows. "Got it?"

He held up his hand. "Got it. I won't *try* anything without your permission." As Kate took his upraised hand and slipped the ring onto his finger, Montana muttered, "I don't *try*...I *do*."

Kate glared at him. "This marriage is fake. Don't forget that."

"Trust me. I won't." Montana leaned forward and pressed his lips to hers in a brief brush of a kiss.

A blast of electricity ripped through Kate, followed by heat, searing a path through her chest and down low in her belly. She pressed her fingers to her lips. "Why did you do that?"

"Only seemed fitting, after tying the knot." He winked, sending another rush of heat rushing through her veins. "Want me to take it back?"

She rubbed the back of her hand over her mouth, her head spinning. "You can't take something like that back. Once given, it can't be returned."

"Oh well, I guess you'll have to keep it." He smiled and sat back against the plush leather seat.

"Well, don't do it again." Thankfully, the car pulled up to the curb at the Baltimore International Airport and dropped them off with their luggage.

Two minutes later, Mica Brantley's limousine arrived, picked them up and drove them back into the city.

Once they'd switched chauffeur-driven vehicles, Kate remained silent, going over the script Tazer had given them. Not only did she have to know the details about the fictitious Lindemanns, she had to be prepared to step into Mica Brantley's shoes at a moment's notice. She had to know Mica's idiosyncrasies, which would be much harder to pull off if they ran into anyone who knew her and Trevor Brantley.

Over an hour since they'd left the shops, the limousine pulled up in front of the Jefferson Hotel, one of the oldest and most expensive hotels in downtown DC. Once Monty and Kayla Lindemann got settled, they were to meet Mrs. Brantley for dinner.

The chauffeur opened the door.

Montana slid out first and then bent to offer his hand to Kate.

Reluctantly, she placed her fingers against his. That same shock of electricity rippled up her arm and showered warmth throughout her body. He had her so stirred up inside, she tripped over the curb.

If Montana hadn't reached out and yanked her into his arms, smashing her against his chest, she'd have fallen face-first on the concrete sidewalk.

Instead, she was crushed to him, his arms like steel bands around her waist. When she got her feet under her, heat rose up her cheeks. "Sorry."

He leaned close and whispered in her ear, "I'm not." Then he hooked her with one of his big, capable hands and waved toward the door. "Ready?"

She nodded, though she couldn't remember ever being so ill-prepared as she was at that moment. What worried her most was that she had no doubt she could play the part required. Keeping her head on straight and not falling even a little bit for the handsome SEAL would be the real challenge.

While the bellman retrieved their luggage, Montana dealt with the reception desk. Royce and Geek had been busy securing reservations, backdating them to make it appear as though Mr. and Mrs. Lindemann had planned their trip to DC weeks ago.

Kate took a moment to casually glance around the lobby, searching for anything that stood out. Suspicious characters, security cameras, lurking staff members…anything that might set off alarm bells in her head.

Fortunately, or unfortunately, nothing did. She spotted the requisite security cameras placed throughout the lobby for the protection of the wealthy guests.

A warm, rough hand curled around her

elbow. “Ready?” Montana’s deep, rich voice filled her ear and spread over her body like melted butter—warm, smooth and penetrating every fiber of her being. She trembled.

How did he do that?

With a nod, she let him lead her through the lobby to the elevator.

Montana pushed the button for the seventh floor and then slipped his arm around her waist. “Feeling better?”

“I wasn’t aware I was feeling poorly.”

“You know…you don’t have a stomach for flying.” He pulled her against him.

“Oh, yes. I feel much better.” Aware of the camera in the upper right corner, she leaned into Montana. The thin fabric of her suit did little to guard her against her body’s reaction to his.

The elevator door slid open. Kate stepped out, afraid if she stayed any longer, her knees would wobble and refuse to hold her up.

Their room was the last door near the end of the hallway. A stairwell was located at the very end, marked with a sign For Emergency Use Only.

Montana ran the key card over the lock and the green light blinked. When he pushed, the door swung open on oiled hinges.

Kate entered first. Expertly decorated, the

suite contained a sitting room, sleeping chamber and a large bathroom with a shower big enough to fit two.

Montana set the briefcase on a desk in the corner and flipped the spring-loaded latches. He opened the case and extracted a small monitor Kate recognized as the kind she'd used to check for surveillance devices. Bugs.

"Do you need to freshen up before we meet with Mica?" Montana asked, as he crossed to her and slipped the monitor into her palm.

"Sure, but you can go first." She leaned up on her toes and pressed a kiss to his lips.

His irises flared and he caught her arm. "I'll only be a minute." Then he kissed her full on the lips.

Reeling from the rush of searing passion from the kiss, Kate stood in the middle of the room until Montana entered the bathroom and closed the door behind him.

Having been warned that they couldn't trust anyone, Kate had to assume even their room could be bugged. Until she swept the room to determine whether or not there were listening devices, she had to play the part.

While Montana took his time in the bathroom, she walked around the room, pretending to examine the decorations, all the while carrying the monitor in her palm. The alarm vibrated against her hand when she neared the nightstand on the right side of the bed. She leaned close and flicked the light on. A tiny metal object clung to the inside of the shade. First bug.

When she walked to the other side of the bed and leaned over the nightstand, the monitor again vibrated in her hand. As she switched on the light, she noted a second bug clinging to the inside of that shade. Walking through every part of the room and the adjoining suite, she located two more listening devices and a miniature camera affixed to the chandelier in the sitting room.

By the time she'd completed a thorough sweep, the bathroom door opened and Montana emerged.

Kate hurried toward him, plastering a smile on her face. She flung her arms around him and pulled his head down for a kiss.

"Mmm. To what do I owe the pleasure?" Montana wrapped his arms around her waist and held her close.

She leaned back. "Do I have to have a reason to kiss my husband?"

"No." He bent and kissed her, then nuzzled her neck. "What's up?"

"Bugs on both nightstands," she whispered in his ear, then nibbled his earlobe. "Mmm.

Maybe we should skip dinner with Mica and stay here for dessert."

"You don't have to twist my arm," Montana responded.

"Camera in the chandelier and two more bugs in the sitting room," she breathed into his ear.

Montana gave her a very slight nod. "Mmm, you smell delicious," he said aloud. Then in a whisper Kate had to strain to hear, he added, "Leave them or destroy?"

Her pulse hammering and her blood burning through her system, Kate struggled to push away from Montana. "We'd better leave. Mica will be expecting us."

"Agreed." He kissed her once more and set her at arm's length. "We can pick up where we left off, later."

Kate's breath hitched in her chest and she hastily turned away before she fell back into the SEAL's strong arms. Just the thought of picking up where they'd left off made her heart skip several beats and then run on like she'd just finished a marathon.

"I need to powder my nose," she said, and dodged into the bathroom. A quick scan with the monitor located one more bug behind the mirror. After she'd located it, she took a moment to stare at her reflection, surprised at what she saw. Never had she looked so much like a model ready to hit the runway. This wasn't the Kate she knew. Nothing about the face staring back at her was familiar. Especially the way she felt inside.

Yes, she could understand her attraction to the SEAL. After all, he was built like a fighting machine, solid and muscular, with the bonus of being ruggedly handsome.

Hadn't she learned her lesson about falling for her partner? She wasn't a brand-new agent with stars in her eyes. Been there… done that…got the demotion to prove it.

Kate applied a fresh coat of lipstick, straightened her shoulders and marched out of the bathroom.

This assignment might prove to be the hardest one she'd ever undertaken. But she'd be damned if she went down without a fight. Even if she was fighting herself.

Chapter Four

Montana's lips still tingled from touching Kate's. He'd been more than tempted to follow through on his threat to ditch Mica and stay in the room with his partner.

When she'd ducked into the bathroom, he'd made his rounds of the suite, without appearing too obvious. All the bugs, and the camera in the chandelier of the sitting room, meant someone had been in there in preparation for their arrival. Since the hotel's computers and Mica's driver had known for less than a couple hours that they were coming, it had to have been an expert job to get all the bugs in so quickly.

These kinds of tactics were foreign to Montana. Give him a gun and a wedge of plastic explosives, and he could blast his way through the enemy. Not here. His adversary was elusive and hid among innocents in a highly populated urban area that didn't see the usual terrorist activities of a war-torn, third-world country.

The sound of the door opening made him turn around.

As when he'd first seen her step out of the high-end clothing salon's back room, Montana's breath caught in his throat. Kate was absolutely beautiful. The skirt suit hugged her body, accentuating every curve to perfection.

Again, he wanted to skip the meeting with Mica and explore the zipper and buttons he'd have to overcome to strip Kate out of the outfit. Then he'd get to her hair, pulling pins and whatever it was that tucked it behind her head in a smooth sweep.

She smiled. "Ready?"

"Yes." More than she'd ever know. He waved his hand, urging her to lead the way through the door, while he adjusted his trousers to accommodate his arousal.

In the hallway, he took her elbow and walked with her to the elevator, selecting the restaurant level, where they would meet Mica.

Kate slipped her hand into his, but remained silent all the way down.

As Montana stepped out of the elevator, the smells of food made his stomach rumble. It wasn't until then that he realized he and Kate hadn't had lunch.

They entered the restaurant and Montana glanced around for Mrs. Brantley.

"I don't see her. Do you?" Kate asked.

"No. Would you like a cocktail while we wait?"

Kate nodded. "Whiskey on the rocks."

He smiled.

Kate frowned. "What?"

"I was thinking something a little more..." He struggled for the right word.

"Fruity? You know me better." She shook her head. "I like my alcohol as strong as my men." Kate tossed her head and strode toward the bar, her hips swaying with each step.

Heat rushed through him and Montana tugged at the tie around his neck, feeling as if he might choke, break a sweat or both. Kate might prove to be more woman than he could handle. Given her training, she might even be able to kick his butt in hand-to-hand combat. The thought of wrestling with Kate made him even hotter.

She ordered her drink and turned to Montana.

"I'll have a Guinness," he said. Liquor dulled his wits. Not that he'd drink the entire beer. He still found it hard to believe they could be in danger. The bar was like any bar in the US. People came in, never expecting to be shot at or have a bomb go off next to them.

The bartender set the drinks on the counter in front of them.

Montana lifted the longneck bottle and touched it to her whiskey glass. "To old friends."

"And new adventures." She tipped the glass and drank a long swallow. "There she is." Kate nodded toward the door.

Mica Brantley entered, wearing a black dress, the neckline dipping low in front, and displaying a sparkling diamond necklace. Her hair was swept up into a smooth bun at the back of her head.

Rex Masters followed her, keeping close enough that he could throw himself in front of anyone who decided to rush the woman. His broad shoulders were a testament to a man who stayed in shape, ready for anything. The bulky lump beneath his jacket had to be a concealed weapon.

Mica glanced around the room. When she spotted them, she smiled and hurried forward. "Kayla, Monty! How wonderful of you to come for the gala."

Kate moved forward and air-kissed both of

Mica's cheeks. "We wouldn't have missed it for the world."

Montana lifted Mica's hand to his lips and kissed her knuckles. He'd seen a secret agent in one of the thriller movies do that with a high-class woman. He hoped it wasn't just something they made up for the movies.

Mica frowned. "Really, Monty?" Holding on to his hand, she pulled him closer and kissed his cheek. "That's better. No need to be formal with me."

Beside him, Kate slid her hand through his bent elbow. "Shall we find a table? We're famished."

"Oh, good. The food here is above par. I've had no complaints anytime I've stayed here."

"How long have you been in town?" Kate asked, keeping up a running conversation.

"Got here today. Since Trevor's…passing, I haven't had the heart to go back to the house."

"I don't blame you. But where have you been staying?"

"Here and there." Mica waved her hand. "I can't seem to settle." Makeup couldn't hide the shadows beneath the woman's eyes. Her husband's death and her driving determination to find the one responsible were taking their toll on Mrs. Brantley.

Montana understood loss of a loved one.

He'd lost more than one of his teammates in firefights. It wasn't something a person got over easily.

The maître d' showed them to their table. As they sat, a familiar voice spoke behind Montana. "Good evening, I'm Dutton. I'll be your server."

Montana fought to keep a grin from spreading across his face. Duff stood straight in a black waiter's uniform, a fringe of gray hair circling his seemingly bald head. Someone had done an expert job of blending makeup into the natural tanned tones of his skin, covering any of the lines from the skullcap wig, all the way around his head.

If Montana hadn't known the voice, he wouldn't have guessed the waiter was Duff. Based on the bland glances from the others at the table, they hadn't caught on to their waiter being one of the other SEALs on the team.

At one point after ordering their dinner, Montana rose under the pretext of going to the restroom. On the way, he caught Duff and asked for another napkin. On a much quieter note, he asked, "Anyone else?"

"The gang's all here," Duff whispered. Louder, he said, "If you'll wait right here, I'll have that napkin to you right away, sir." He spun on his heels, ducked behind a partition and returned with a cloth napkin. "Here you go, sir. Let me know if there's anything else I can do for you." Duff winked. "All you have to do is ask." He pressed the napkin into Montana's hand and squeezed.

Montana could feel something more than the napkin being pressed into his palm. He nodded. "Thank you." He folded the napkin, tucked it into his inside pocket and continued toward the bathroom.

Once inside the beautifully equipped oasis, he entered a stall, pulled out the napkin and carefully unfolded it. Inside was a small, flesh-toned earbud radio headset. He pressed it deep into his ear canal and listened.

Sawyer's voice came online. "Comm check."

"Rip here."

"Duff here."

"Loverboy here."

"Hunter here."

At that moment, the swish of a door opening and footsteps sounded. Knowing it was his turn to check in, Montana pressed the lever on the toilet at the same time as he said, "Monty here." He stepped out of the stall and crossed to the sink.

Whoever had entered the restroom had gone straight into one of the stalls and closed the door.

Sawyer continued, "All present and accounted for."

Montana washed his hands quickly and dried them, then stepped out of the restroom into the empty hallway.

"Geek has Lance and me positioned in a van outside the Jefferson," Sawyer said. "We're tapped into the hotel security system, but keep your eyes open."

"The monitoring device Montana had in his room recorded six bugs," Geek said. "We backed up the security footage on the hotel corridors and stairwells. There was a freeze-frame at two points today. Those two points were between the time Mrs. Brantley made arrangements for her car to pick up the Lindemanns at the airport, and the time they arrived two hours later." He paused. "Just to be clear...if things go south, our primary goal is to get Mrs. Brantley out alive."

Knowing his team had his six in the hotel, Montana felt better, less exposed, not like a sitting duck, waiting for something to happen. His buddies would be watching all angles, checking for anyone acting strange.

Back at the dinner table, Montana studied Mica's bodyguard. He'd been with her in Cancun when they'd blown open the human trafficking auction and rescued the women who were to be sold to the highest bidder.

Though Rex sat with them at the table, he didn't contribute to the conversation, except when Mica included him. Then he answered in cryptic responses. His gaze moved around the room constantly. Having chosen the seat with his back to the wall, he had a one-hundred-eighty-degree view of the dining room and its occupants.

Montana sat with his back to the door, not liking it one bit. But with Duff moving in and out, delivering food and drinks, he wasn't as worried.

Mrs. Brantley and Kate talked through dinner about their fake travels together in Paris and the upcoming gala at the yacht club.

Halfway through the meal, Mica passed a key card to Montana beneath the table. He assumed it was to her room, should they need it. He slid it into his trouser pocket.

When the meal was over, Montana was glad to stand and look around. The tables had filled with well-dressed businessmen and ladies wearing cocktail dresses, none of whom appeared to be spies or traitors ready to gun down Mica Brantley. But one never knew. Bad guys came in all shapes and sizes. Sometimes they were children with explosives strapped around them, sent into the middle of a group of soldiers.

The question roiling around in Montana's mind was, why was all the surveillance added to their room? Were the people stalking Mrs. Brantley trying to get to her through her friends?

Some things didn't make any sense in this case. Montana wished he could have an open discussion with Kate and Mrs. Brantley. Mrs. Brantley because she was the potential target. Kate because this was the kind of work she'd been trained for.

Frustrated and determined to get answers, Montana bided his time, acting as if he enjoyed the inane conversation about acquaintances Mrs. Brantley expected to see the next day at the club, and the usual big donors.

Montana made mental notes about the names Mrs. Brantley brought up, in case they ran across them at the gala. Tomorrow would be a more hectic day, trying to keep track of Mrs. Brantley and make sure she wasn't attacked, or that the politicians and wealthy donors weren't harmed. If Montana had his way, he'd have had the gala rescheduled. Or at the very least, he would encourage Mrs. Brantley to skip it.

All four of them entered the elevator together, along with two more of Mrs. Brantley's bodyguards. They rode to the seventh floor, where Montana and Kate got off, bidding Mrs. Brantley good-evening.

Once in their room, Montana still couldn't relax. Knowing they were being bugged and watched didn't help. He took off the suit jacket and tossed it over the back of a chair.

Kate unbuttoned her jacket. "It was good seeing Mica again, don't you think?"

"Mmm, yes." He stepped up behind her and helped her out of the jacket. "But it would be even better to see you naked in the shower." He felt her stiffen. Montana nibbled on her earlobe and whispered, "We can talk with the water on."

She nodded, leaned her head back and turned her mouth to kiss his neck. "The only way that's going to happen is to get out of these clothes." She cupped his cheek and pulled him down for a kiss on the lips. Then she stepped away from him, walking out of the jacket he held on to. "What are you waiting for?"

Montana grinned. "For my brain to engage." After hanging up her garment, he jerked the tie loose from around his neck and threw it toward the jacket on the back of the chair. It landed somewhere on the floor. Montana didn't care. He had to remind himself that Kate's come-on was an act, but it had the same effect as her come-hither looks would if they'd been real. He followed like a starving man to a smorgasbord.

Once inside the bathroom, they wouldn't have to keep up the pretense of stripping, but they had to be aware of the listening device located behind the mirror.

Montana turned on the faucet, giving it as much pressure as it would allow. The more water blasting into the shower stall, the better it would cover the sound of their voices.

When he turned, he was stunned to see Kate standing in nothing but her panties and bra.

"Need help getting undressed?" she asked.

"No, I just need to get protection. Unless, of course, you're ready to start a family."

She laughed. "Maybe in a year or two."

"Here, let me unclip your bra," Montana said for their listeners. He pulled the radio from his ear and held it up for her to see.

Her eyes widened and then she nodded. "Last one in is a rotten egg." She stepped into the shower, still wearing her bra and panties.

Montana stripped off everything and dug a condom out of his wallet. He didn't know where being naked with Kate might lead, but, by damned, he'd be prepared. Wrapping a towel around his waist, he stepped into the shower.

Kate had taken the pins out of her hair and applied shampoo. "I thought you had changed your mind," she said, loudly enough to be heard over the spray. Her eyes were closed to the soap bubbles running down her face and over her shoulders.

Montana set the foil package in the soap dish, trying but failing to keep his gaze from following the path of the bubbles as they dipped into the cups hugging the CIA agent's breasts. He stood with one hand holding the corners of the towel, regretting that he'd had to strip out of the expensive trousers. Seeing Kate almost naked had the natural effect of tenting the towel. He adjusted, holding the towel loosely, praying she didn't notice. *Fat chance.*

KATE COULD SENSE when Montana stepped into the shower. Not so much by the sounds, but by the way her body heated at his mere presence. Lowering her voice so that only Montana could hear, she said, "I had to get all the pins and hair spray out. It was making my scalp itch."

"Good. I like your hair down better," he

said, his voice deliciously warm, like the water caressing her body. She wished she could have taken off her bra and panties and melted into Montana's rock-hard muscles. The man was tempting her more than her former partner ever had.

Kate wasn't the same naive newbie, green from school with stars in her eyes. She was a grown woman, with needs like any other red-blooded female. Sex didn't require giving her heart or trust to the man. Surely she could keep those separate. What would it hurt to play this role all the way? The Lindemanns were a married couple. Making love in a hotel would be the natural thing to do, especially when they were in a shower, supposedly naked.

Her channel clenched and an ache built deep in her core.

She tried to tell herself that lusting after the SEAL wasn't getting the case solved. It would only get in the way of clear thinking and lightning reflexes.

She rinsed her hair, feeling the warm water rushing over her sensitized breasts and down her torso to soak her panties. Maybe she'd be better off giving in to her lust, seducing the SEAL and getting him out of her system.

Kate rinsed the suds out of her hair, braced

herself to keep from giving away her carnal thoughts and blinked open her eyes.

Her glance swept over Montana, pausing on the tented towel. Heat rushed into her cheeks as she realized he was just as aroused. She jerked her gaze up to his and anchored there. "What's happening?" That was the question of the century. Hell, she knew what was happening between them, but she had to get her mind out of the towel and onto the case.

Montana's lips twitched at the corners. Speaking in a low, sexy tone, he said, "My team is here. They're tapped into the hotel security system and they're monitoring all movements in and out."

Even though Montana was only filling her in on his team's activities, Kate couldn't help the shiver of awareness trickling down her spine along with the warm soapy water. She drew in a steadying breath. "Good. Anything unusual?"

"They're concerned about us, since our room was bugged," he said, his hand shifting. Water drenched the towel, plastering it to his thighs and emphasizing his long, thick erection.

Holy hell. She wanted to reach out and

touch him there, to take the towel from his hands and fling it to the shower floor.

"I don't care about us," Kate said, when it was far from the truth. She cared what would happen *between* them, not *to* them. "I'm worried about Mrs. B." Kate crossed her arms over her chest. "She's been here less than a day. It might be only a matter of time before someone goes after her."

"Based on the dates and coordinates, she might be the target for tomorrow's charity gala."

"That list was created before the events in Cancun. Everything could have changed. A new list could be out, or whoever is orchestrating the killings might have adjusted his schedule accordingly. Hell, he might be shooting from the hip now that he knows someone is looking for him and possibly getting closer."

"True. All the more reason to keep our eyes and ears open." Montana shifted, bumping into her.

That slight touch set off a spark of electricity that turned into a fire raging all the way through to her very core. Much more togetherness and she'd be helpless to resist.

Kate stepped back quickly. Her foot slipped on the tiles and she pitched forward.

Montana let go of the towel he'd been holding and grabbed her around her waist, pulling her against him to steady her. His hardened staff pressed into her belly.

The air caught in Kate's lungs and refused to move in or out. "Um, thanks," she said.

"No problem," Montana replied through tight lips.

For a moment, they stared into each other's eyes.

"I guess it's not a secret that I find you incredibly attractive," he said, his erection shifting between them.

If possible, it was getting even longer and harder. Desperate to breathe, Kate sucked in some air, her body moving with the effort, her belly sliding ever so slightly over that velvety smooth, hard shaft between them.

Again, her lungs seized and her knees wobbled. Kate gripped his arms to stabilize herself. "Mmm. This could get awkward."

"Or not." His hands tightened around her waist. "We're supposed to be a married couple."

"But we're not," she reminded him and herself. "We're on a case, not vacation."

He nodded. "You're right."

When he started to back away, she tightened her grip, her hands responding to her body's desire, while her mind yelled, *What the hell are you doing?*

"I'm confused," he said. "When a woman says she's not interested, I don't push the issue."

"I didn't say I wasn't interested." She wet her suddenly dry lips. The shower spray was cooling, but did little to chill the passion raging inside Kate.

Montana's fingers flexed against her skin. "I'm just a cowboy from Montana. Be clear in what you want, or I let go and walk away."

The direct and searing look in his blue eyes bored through her resolve. Hell, who was she kidding? Kate couldn't walk away from what was happening between them. *Get it over with*, she told herself. *Get him out of your system, and get back to work.*

"We don't have much time," she said. "We don't know when or if someone will make a move."

"Darlin', time should never be the issue." He raised his hand to the back of her bra and flicked the hooks free. "Where there's a will, there's a way." He peeled the straps down her arms and flung the garment over the top of the shower stall. Then he hooked his fingers into her panties and dragged them down her legs.

When he reached her ankles, Kate couldn't wait a moment longer. She kicked the panties to the side. "Got protection?"

Montana nodded and straightened. As he did, he cupped her buttocks, lifted and pressed her back against the cool tiles. "Would you believe me if I told you I was a Boy Scout?"

"Mmm." She wiggled her bottom, inching downward toward his jutting staff. "I'm not in the habit of making love to a Boy Scout." She pressed her finger to his lips. "A little less talk, please."

"Got it." He grabbed the foil packet from the soap dish.

She snatched it from his hand, tore it open and applied it, all in a few swift, efficient moves. "Now, show me what you're made of." God, this was really going to happen. She was going to make love with a man she'd met only that morning. Either she was a fool or she was one gutsy, empowered female, taking her sexual needs and desires by the horn and riding them to the end.

She cupped his face between her palms and bent to capture his lips with hers. He obliged with no resistance, pushing his tongue past her teeth to caress hers in a long, slow glide she hoped would be his style when he entered her.

Whatever she was, she was hot, needy and impatient to consummate their fake marriage.

Chapter Five

Montana captured Kate's wrists in one of his hands and pressed them to the tile above her head. Then he crushed her mouth, kissing her hard, as if he could draw the breath from her into him.

With his shaft poised at her opening, he rocked his hips, dipping into her slick wetness.

Kate wrapped her legs around his waist and dug her heels into his buttocks, urging him to go deeper.

He complied, sliding in a little more, allowing her channel to adjust to his girth. He knew he was built a little bigger than most men, based on observation in the shower room. He didn't want to hurt her.

"More," Kate moaned. "Want more."

He inched deeper, glad for the water and the slickness of her juices lubricating his way.

With every ounce of control he could muster, he held back, determined to take her slowly.

"Please," she begged. "Give me all you've got." Her thighs tightened and her heels dug into him, pulling him closer, harder, deeper.

"I don't want to hurt you," he whispered into her mouth.

She nibbled his bottom lip and sucked it between her teeth. When she let go, she said, "I can handle it. Do it. Now." She sank down on him, her channel clenching around him.

His control slipped and he thrust deep, pushing all the way to the hilt. She felt good, wrapped around him, hot, tight and wet. Montana remained buried inside her, letting her adjust to his size for several long seconds, then he moved out and back in.

Her legs contracted and she fought to free her wrists. "Let go. I want to touch you." When he released his grip, she laid her hands on his shoulders, digging her nails into his skin as she rode him.

Montana pumped in and out, faster and faster until the sensations culminated in a rush of adrenaline and white-hot heat surging throughout his body. Starting in his shaft, surges rippled outward as he shot over the edge and rocketed into the heavens.

He thrust one last time and held her hips

tight against him, as wave after wave consumed him.

When he came back to earth, he drew in a deep breath and leaned his forehead against hers. "Incredible."

"Yes," she said, her breathing ragged.

The cool water and wrinkled skin reminded Montana of just how long they'd been in the shower. He eased Kate to her feet, pulling out of her. Discarding the condom, he picked up the bar of soap, worked up a lather and glanced at her questioningly.

A smile spread across her lips and she raised her arms.

He started with her hands, running his soapy fingers over her arms and downward to the swells of her breasts. Pausing for a moment, he tweaked and teased the distended nipples until they hardened into little beads. Leaning her beneath the cooling water, he let the spray rinse away the bubbles, then he caught one nipple between his teeth and rolled it until she squirmed against him.

She grasped his head in her hands and moved him to the other nipple.

He tongued and flicked the tip until Kate's back arched and she moaned.

Sucking her breast into his mouth, he ran his hand down her torso, over her belly and lower, to the mound of hair at the apex of her thighs.

Her chest rose on a deep, indrawn breath and her hips pushed forward.

Encouraged, Montana slid his fingers between her folds and touched the little strip of flesh there.

Her hips rocked hard against him and she groaned.

Montana flicked and then skimmed a finger over the sensitive nubbin.

Kate dug her fingers into the hair at the nape of his neck. "Yes. There," she whispered.

He dipped his finger into her and stroked her with his thumb at the same time.

Her body quivered against his and she widened her legs.

Dragging his damp finger upward, he swirled and teased until she grew rigid in his arms, her breathing halted and she squeezed her eyes shut.

Then she cupped her hand over his, pressing hard as she rocked her hips. For a long moment he held her there, letting her ride her release all the way to the end. When she sagged against him, he rinsed them both, turned off the cold water and stepped out of the shower stall.

With a plush, terry-cloth towel, he rubbed the moisture from her body and hair, kissing her shoulder, neck and breasts as he worked.

Armed with a dry towel, Kate returned the favor until they were both dry and naked in the bathroom.

Montana wrapped her in a towel and wound one around himself. He mouthed the word, *"Ready?"*

She nodded.

Montana planted the radio in his ear and stepped out of the bathroom, carrying a hand towel. With a quick snap, he tossed the towel over the camera on the chandelier in the sitting room.

"Mmm," Kate said. "That's nice." She made it sound like he was kissing her, or making love to her again, but he knew she meant it was nice they could dress without someone watching.

In the bedroom, Kate skipped the beautiful negligee and sheer nightgown and opted for Montana's pajama top. Drawing it over her head, she let it fall over her body to hang down to midthigh. Then she pulled on a clean pair of panties from her suitcase.

Montana watched her dress, enjoying every movement. Kate made putting on clothes as sexy as taking them off. If he hadn't just spent himself in the shower, he'd consider making love to her all over again.

Instead, he dressed in pajama bottoms. Nothing else. He figured it was better than sleeping in the nude, wondering if they'd missed a camera somewhere. He had to admit he kind of liked it that Kate wore the other half of his nightclothes. It made her seem more real to him than the made-up Mrs. Lindemann.

Kate glanced at the bed. "Should we attempt to get some sleep?" she asked.

"The gala lasts a good portion of tomorrow evening, so we'll need all the rest we can get," Montana replied.

Kate nodded and slipped into the bed, pulling the sheet and duvet up to her waist.

Montana sat on the edge, his staff hardening at the thought of sleeping with the beautiful CIA agent. If something didn't happen soon, he'd be making love to her again, and maybe all night long.

As he swung his legs up into the bed, something popped in the suite. Montana leaped to his feet. "Did you hear that?"

Kate was out of the bed and on her feet in a flash. "I did. What do you suppose it could be?"

Montana shrugged. "Stay here. I'll check it out."

As he neared the doorway to the sitting area, his heart started racing at the same time as his skin grew cold.

"Sweetheart," he said. "You might want to get dressed. I smell smoke."

Kate joined Montana in the doorway, dragging one of the hotel bathrobes over her shoulders. She scanned the room with its antique sofa and Martha Washington secretary desk against one wall. "Where?"

Montana pointed. "There." He hurried toward an electrical socket. Smoke rose from the holes in the plate, spiraling upward.

Kate hurried around the room, looking in the coat closet near the door, checking behind armchairs. "If we had an extinguisher..."

Montana ran for the telephone and punched the zero. "We have a faulty electrical socket that just caught fire. Please send someone up with a fire extinguisher, and notify the fire department. ASAP."

In the next second, the alarm system went off, the incessant whine filling the hallway outside their room.

"That's our cue to get out of here." Montana ran for the bedroom, shucked his pajamas and dragged on his jeans and shoes.

"Should we grab our things?" Kate asked.

"Leave them. We can replace things. You can't replace people."

Kate tied a robe around her pajama top, jammed her feet into a pair of slippers and ran for the door.

Montana was there first. He leaned close and whispered in her ear, "We're going up."

She glanced at him, her eyes wide. "Up?"

He nodded and murmured, "This could be a ploy to draw Mica out of her room." Louder, he said, "Ready?"

Kate nodded. "Ready."

He opened the door and looked before he stepped out. Two couples emerged from other rooms down the hall, heading for the elevator. As expected, the elevators weren't running. They turned toward the stairs as Montana shut the door behind him and waited for them to go ahead. Once they'd passed and entered the stairwell, he tapped the ear with the headset. "Talk to me."

"Where have you been?" Sawyer said. "Never mind, someone set off the fire alarm."

"That would be because of the fire I reported in an electrical socket in our suite," Montana said.

"That explains it. I suspect things are about to get crazy. I'm scrambling the cameras on seven and eight. You know where you need to go."

"Going." Montana grabbed Kate's hand and ran for the stairwell. Instead of going down with the other couples, they turned and climbed to the next level. Using the spare key card Mrs. Brantley had passed to him beneath the dining table, Montana was able to gain access to the penthouse floor. He hurried toward the Martha Jefferson Suite. If Mica and Rex were still there, they'd need to get out soon. And they'd need all of them to keep Mrs. Brantley safe from whoever was after her.

KATE'S PULSE RACED as she ran toward the door to Mica's suite.

Montana swept the card over the reader. The green light blinked on and he pushed the door inward. A shot rang out, hitting the wall on the other side of the hall.

Kate's blood ran cold. Had Montana charged straight in, he'd have been hit in the head. Without weapons, they couldn't shoot back. But they couldn't stand out in the corridor, waiting for the shooter to kill Mica. Assuming he hadn't already.

"We have a shooter in the Brantley room,"

Montana said softly. "Could use some backup. I'm going in."

"I am, too," Kate added.

Montana glanced across the open doorway at her. He opened his mouth to say something, seemed to think better of it and shrugged. "Just don't give him a target. Okay?"

"Okay."

Montana dived into the sitting room of the suite and rolled behind a couch.

Kate drew in a deep breath and somersaulted into the room, rolling to a stop behind an antique sofa. Feeling naked without her gun, she waited and listened before calling out, "Mica? Rex?"

A loud crash sounded in another room, as if someone had broken a window.

Montana leaped to his feet and ran into the next room. "He's getting away," he called out.

Kate raced into a beautifully equipped bedroom. One of the windows had been broken. Montana leaned through the broken glass.

"The bastard went out the window," Rex Masters called out from a corner on the other side of the bed. He held his arm close to his chest, blood oozing from beneath his elbow.

Kate ran toward him. "Where's Mica?"

"Barricaded in the bathroom. Don't let him

get away." He tossed his gun to Kate with his free hand. "I'm hit, or I'd go after him myself."

Montana grabbed a pillow from the bed, tore off the case and wrapped the ends around each hand. Then he was back at the window. "Cover me."

Before Kate could respond, Montana was over the ledge, walking backward down the side of the eight-story building, holding on to a thin cable with his hands wrapped in the pillowcase.

The shadowy figure farther down the cable leaped to the ground and pointed a gun up at Montana.

Kate leaned out as far as she could and fired down at the man on the ground. A bullet whizzed past her head, splintering the window frame above her.

Montana was halfway down the cable when someone burst into the room behind Kate.

She swung around and aimed at the waiter who'd worked their table earlier that evening. He carried a gun and had it pointing at her.

"It's me, Duff," he said.

Kate nodded. "Good." She tucked the gun into her robe pocket, grabbed a pillowcase and wrapped her hands in it. "Stay with them and cover us."

"Where are you going?" Duff asked.

"After Monty." Before Duff could stop her, Kate stepped out onto the ledge, lowered herself over the side and gripped the cable with her wrapped hands. Easing her way downward, she prayed she didn't lose her grip. As she slid toward the ground, her hands grew hotter and hotter, the pillowcase wearing through to her skin before she reached the bottom. She glanced behind her, watching the direction Montana took off as he hit the ground.

Anxious to be there, too, Kate dropped the last ten feet to avoid blistering her hands. She rolled to her feet, pulled the gun from her pocket and took off after the two men.

It wasn't long before she kicked off the slippers and ran barefoot across the street and through a back alley.

Gunfire sounded from around the side of a building.

Her heart hammering against her ribs and her breath coming in gasps, she slowed at the corner and peered around.

A man stood at the next corner. Between him and Kate sat a large industrial trash bin. A movement at the base of the bin caught her attention.

It was Montana, crouched low.

The man at the other end of the alley fired. A bullet pinged off the bin.

Apparently, the shooter hadn't noticed Kate yet.

He fired again. The shot ricocheted off the pavement next to Montana.

Kate aimed down the barrel of the unfamiliar pistol Rex had thrown at her and fired. At that exact moment, the shooter turned and ran around the corner. Whether or not her bullet had hit him, she didn't know.

Montana turned. "Kate? What the hell?"

"He's getting away," she called out, running toward the other end of the building.

As she came abreast of Montana, he caught her around the waist and stopped her.

"Why are you stopping me?" she cried, fighting against his hold. "He'll get away."

"Give me the gun. You stay here, and I'll go after him."

"Fine." She shoved the pistol into his hands. "Go."

Montana took off after the gunman. When he reached the corner, he stopped.

Kate ran to catch up. "Why did you stop?"

"He's gone."

"Gone?" She started past him.

Montana's hand shot out. "A car took off with him in it. Trust me, he's gone. All I saw was the flash of taillights." He put the pistol on Safe and tucked it into his trouser pocket.

Now that she had stopped, Kate bent over, bracing her hands on her knees, fighting to catch her breath after the headlong race to catch up to the gunman.

"Damn it, Kate."

She glanced up, still struggling to catch her breath. "What?"

He pointed at her feet. "Where the hell are your shoes?" Before she could answer, Montana swept her up into his arms.

"They slowed me down." She wiggled her feet and tugged at the robe as it fell open, exposing most of her thigh. "Put me down. I can walk."

"Your feet are cut and bleeding."

She frowned, noticing for the first time he was right and her feet were cut, her big toe bleeding from the tip. "You'll be cut and bleeding if you don't put me down," she said, with a little less steam than she was aiming for. Now that she wasn't running after Montana, determined to save the unarmed idiot from being shot, she had time to think about her feet and how they were tender, scratched and bloody. Still…he didn't have to carry her back to the hotel.

He pressed his lips to hers in a brief kiss. "Just hush and let me be the man."

"You *are* the man," she said, her lips tingling. "But that doesn't mean you have to *man*handle me."

Montana shook his head, but held on to her and kept walking back to the hotel. "Do you ever stop talking?"

"Do you ever do as you're told?" she retorted.

"Only if it's the right thing." He stopped next to a van parked against the curb on a street a block from the Jefferson Hotel.

"Why did you stop?" she asked, and looked around.

He tapped his ear. "Open the van door."

The back door opened and Sawyer leaned out. "Damn it, Montana. Why the hell did you let him get away?" He reached for Kate and lifted her into the van. "How are you, Miss McKenzie?"

"Fine, except when your teammate decides I can't walk on my own two feet."

He set her on a cushioned office chair in front of an array of electronics and monitors. "And those two feet are pretty messed up." He reached into a cabinet over his head and extracted a first-aid kit.

Sirens sounded nearby, wailing toward them.

Kate craned her neck, searching for a window. "How do you see outside?"

"Through the camera." Sawyer pointed to a screen.

The monitor displayed the front of the Jefferson Hotel. Guests milled around in the street, some dressed in suits or cocktail dresses, others in bathrobes. A first responder fire truck raced by and stopped in front of the hotel. Men jumped out and ran into the building. A long-ladder truck sped by and halted in the middle of the street. Firefighters leaped to the ground and pulled hoses from the sides of the truck.

A figure dressed in a hotel bellboy uniform ran across the street headed for the van. A second later a knock sounded.

"Let Hunter in," Sawyer said, without turning away from the first-aid kit.

"Here." Montana took the alcohol pads from him. "Let me do this. You're supposed to be on the monitors."

"I got it covered," Lance, the SOS computer guy, said from a seat on the other end of the van.

Sawyer opened the door and Hunter leaped aboard. "We need to pick up a special delivery on the dock at the back of the Jefferson before the streets in and out are complete blocked."

Sawyer climbed into the front seat. "Hold on to your hats." He shifted into gear and drove through the gathering crowd of emergency personnel and hotel guests, turned on the side street leading to the back of the hotel and backed up to the loading dock.

Hunter flung open the rear door of the van.

A balding man with a gray fringe pushed a laundry cart full of sheets toward them. Flanking him were two more members of the SEAL team. Kate recognized them as Quentin and Rip.

Everyone crowded deeper into the communications van, making room for the laundry cart.

As soon as the door closed on all eight of the team and the cart, Duff, the balding man with the fringe, shouted, "Go!"

Sawyer hit the accelerator, sending the van shooting out into the street, heading away from the Jefferson Hotel and into the heart of DC.

At the first stoplight, the sheets shifted and a man's head emerged from beneath.

"Are we clear?" Rex Masters asked.

"Bring her up," Duff said. He pulled the sheets aside until a slim hand reached out.

He grasped it and helped Mica Brantley out of the cart.

The light changed and the van surged forward.

Rex lurched and crashed into Rip and Quentin.

Duff caught Mica and held her steady.

"We need to get Rex to a doctor," she said.

"Royce has one on the way to our disaster recovery site," Lance informed them. "That's where we're headed now."

Kate glanced up at Montana, who calmly swayed with the motion of the van and applied a bandage to her cut toe.

Amid the commotion and insanity of the crowded van, he was Kate's rock, grounding her to a new reality. Once her toe was bandaged, he slipped his arm around her and held on until the van pulled up to an automatic overhead door. When it opened, the van pulled in and the door closed behind them, shutting out the traffic, lights and noise that was a twenty-four-hour part of Washington, DC.

Kate drew in a deep breath and leaned into Montana's quiet strength, glad he was her partner for this mission. Whatever the next day brought she could handle, as long as he was by her side. The man had her back.

Chapter Six

When the van came to a complete stop deep in the bowels of a subterranean parking garage, Montana held on tightly to Kate's hand. One by one, the occupants of the vehicle jumped down. Quentin and Rip each took a side and helped Rex out, half dragging, half carrying him through a doorway into a lit building.

The last ones out, Montana jumped down and held up his arms for Kate.

For once she didn't argue. Instead, she allowed him to lift her into his arms and carry her inside.

He liked holding her close. Sure, the ground inside the alternate SOS work site was swept clean of glass and debris found on city streets, but her feet had taken a beating when she'd chased after him. Whatever had possessed her to run through the streets barefoot, wearing nothing more than a bathrobe and not much else, had Montana shaking his head.

The woman was dedicated, that was certain. At least she had a robe to keep her warm.

Montana had taken time to slip into jeans and his shoes, but he hadn't stopped to throw on a shirt. No longer running, his body had cooled in the damp night air. The sooner they got new clothes, the better.

The team trickled past a guard and entered a corridor. Fontaine stood at the end, waving them into a room. "Hurry. We need to debrief and get some sleep before tomorrow. We have a lot to do." He pointed to Quentin and Rip, who had Rex leaning heavily on them for support, his face pale beneath his rugged tan.

"Take Mr. Masters into the infirmary two doors down. I have a doctor waiting to examine and treat him."

Rip and Quentin continued on to the room indicated and disappeared with the injured man.

"The rest of you can gather here in the conference room," Royce said.

Mica Brantley stopped in front of Fontaine. "I'm sorry we didn't get him this time. We didn't expect an attack from outside of the building."

"Blame that on me." Fontaine patted her

hand. "We should have had surveillance on that side of the hotel. I'm just glad you and Rex are okay."

"I hope Rex will be okay. He took a hit to his side." She glanced toward the doorway down the hall.

"I'd like to have you in the debrief, since Rex is indisposed at this time."

"Anything I can do to help, I will." Mrs. Brantley entered the room.

Fontaine stopped Montana and Kate as they started through the door. "I can't let Mrs. Brantley continue to present herself as bait." He spoke in low tones none of the others could hear from the room beyond. "I need you two to step in."

Montana nodded. He understood what that meant. He and Kate would attend the yacht club gala the following day as Mica Brantley and her bodyguard, Rex Masters.

Tazer appeared. "Don't worry, I had the concierge collect yours and Mrs. Brantley's wardrobes from the hotel. Fortunately, the sprinkler system and smoke didn't damage the contents of your suitcases." She handed Montana a faded black T-shirt. "Sorry, this was all I had in my workout bag. You'll have to put up with Led Zeppelin. If you don't like him, sue me. I'm a huge fan." She waved toward the table. "We'll work on other alternatives after the meeting."

For the next hour, they went over the sequence of events that led to their failed attempt to capture the assassin who'd broken into Mica Brantley's room at the Jefferson. If Mica hadn't been in the bathroom at the time of the invasion, it might not have ended the way it had. Rex Masters had put up a valiant defense.

The attacker had scaled the eight-story building, shooting a cable up to the window ledge and using an automatic lifting device to get him to the top in a hurry.

"That technology isn't readily available to just anyone. Whoever it was had connections," Lance said.

After Mica Brantley imparted what she knew, she stood. "If you're done with me, I'd like to check on Rex."

She left the room and the others continued until there was nothing more to say.

Montana studied Kate during the exchange. She leaned forward, listening intently to the others as they discussed what they'd observed from the different points of view and angles, from the guys in the communications van to those inside the hotel, working as staff members. Since the attack had come from an angle none of them had considered possible, they compared notes and decided they couldn't count on the next day being any easier.

"We'd better get some sleep. Those of you signing on as waitstaff will want to be in place early in the morning," Fontaine said. "I have a team of bomb-sniffing dogs making a pass through the yacht club premises tomorrow morning," the SOS leader continued. "I want to be there when they go through. You all have your assignments. We'll convene in the morning."

The team split up. Lance showed the SEALs to a room farther down the corridor, where cots had been set up and a shower was available.

Fontaine pulled Montana and Kate aside. They entered the infirmary, where they found Rex lying on an examination table with Mrs. Brantley at his side, and a man in a white lab coat tying off a stitch in the patient's side.

The doctor cut the strand, bandaged the wound and gave Rex a bottle of pills. "These are antibiotics. Take them until you run out. You don't want that wound getting infected." The doctor washed his hands in a nearby sink and nodded toward Fontaine. "Let me know if you need further assistance."

"I hope I won't have to call you." Fontaine

held out his hand and shook the doctor's. "Thanks, Cal. I owe you one."

"Don't mention it," the doctor said. "One day I might need your services."

"I hope you won't, but if you do—" Fontaine squeezed the man's hand "—you know you can count on me."

Once the doctor left the room, Fontaine turned to the four of them. "Mica, you can't go to the gala tomorrow."

Rex sat on the edge of the examination table, his face pale, his hand pressed to the bandage on his side. "Agreed."

Mrs. Brantley's lips thinned into a straight line. "I refuse to be intimidated and forced to go into hiding."

"It's temporary, until we find the one responsible," Fontaine assured her.

Mica spun on her heel and paced across the narrow room, turned and paced to stand in front of Fontaine. "My husband has been gone for weeks. I've been in hiding and searching for his killer all that time. Do you call that temporary?"

Fontaine captured her arms in his hands. "I'm sorry this is happening to you, but going to the gala tomorrow is like painting a big bull's-eye on you. We had fewer people to sift through at the hotel today, and someone still got inside. We can't take the chance with hundreds of people at the club and multiple entry points."

Mrs. Brantley lifted her chin. "What if I want to take that chance?"

Montana admired the woman's spunk, but going to the gala was too dangerous. He shifted his gaze to Kate. Taking Mica's place would set her up as the target. Granted, she was a highly trained operative who could probably handle herself in hand-to-hand combat, but she couldn't stop a bullet. And he doubted she'd consider wearing a bulletproof vest beneath her Gucci dress or Prada blouse.

Rex slid off the examination table and swayed slightly. "If you're going, I'm going."

Mrs. Brantley's brows descended. "You can't. You're wounded. You should be in bed, recuperating."

"I go where you go, ma'am."

The widow's frown deepened. "I won't allow it."

Rex's jaw tightened. "You won't have a choice."

"I'll...I'll fire you," she said. Pushing back her shoulders, she stared into her bodyguard's eyes.

Montana knew what Rex's response would be before he put it into words.

"It won't change a thing. I'd still be there to protect you."

Montana had to admire the man's resolve, considering he looked like he was about to pass out on the floor. Blood loss had a way of doing that to you. Montana had seen some of his buddies running on adrenaline. When the action was over, and they realized they'd been wounded and lost a lot of blood, they dropped like a ton of bricks. Montana moved closer to Rex, just in case the man took a dive to the stone-cold concrete floor.

Mrs. Brantley opened her mouth to argue. Apparently, the hard stare she received from Rex made her think again. She snapped her mouth shut and turned to Fontaine. "If I don't go, will that stop the attack on the gala?"

The SOS leader shook his head. "We can't guarantee it. We are assuming the dates and coordinates had something to do with you. But the truth is, the guest list is a who's who of financial and political heavy hitters. They could be the ones targeted, not you."

"Shouldn't we call it off?"

"We have heavy security in place in and around the club," Fontaine said. "What I want to propose is Kate and Montana taking your places as guests."

"As the Lindemanns?" Mrs. Brantley's

brows twisted. "I thought you'd already arranged for them to attend."

Fontaine shook his head. "Not as the Lindemanns but as you and Rex."

Already the widow was shaking her head. "I can't let you do that. I won't let Kate and Montana take a bullet, or an explosive device detonating on them, when it should have been me."

"Ma'am, this kind of work is our job," Kate assured her. "We know what to be on the lookout for and what to do if things go south."

Mrs. Brantley shook her head. "I won't let you or anyone else be hurt on my account. No."

"They're going to be there, anyway," Fontaine insisted. "Going as you will give them the advantage of trust. The people who have come for the past decade are used to seeing your face at the event. They trust you and might talk to you."

"Me." Mrs. Brantley tapped her chest. "They would talk to me."

"We can make Kate look like you, wire her with a radio headset and body cam. You will see what she sees, hear what she hears, and can feed information to her to engage others."

Mica stared at Fontaine, her eyes narrowing. "I thought that was something that could only be done in the movies."

Royce laughed. "That technology is available and works quite well."

She turned to Kate. "And you're willing to do this? To go as me to a gala you know nothing about? To possibly be a target for a bullet you don't deserve?"

Kate nodded and smiled. "Beats pulling desk duty."

Montana almost laughed, but the seriousness of the situation made him hold back.

Finally, Mrs. Brantley drew in a deep breath and let it out slowly. "Okay. I'll agree on one condition."

Royce grinned. "What condition?"

Mrs. Brantley touched Kate's arm with a sad smile. "You keep this lovely young woman alive at all costs. The killing has already taken too great a toll of lives."

Montana's heart clenched. He stepped forward. "That's my job." Raising a hand like he had when he'd sworn into the Navy, he said, "I promise."

"Hey." Kate took Mrs. Brantley's hand. "I'm pretty good at looking out for myself. I'm an expert in hand-to-hand combat. Even if I wasn't, I have all of Mr. Fontaine's resources looking out for me. I'll be okay, as long as I have you in my ear telling me what to say and do."

The widow squeezed Kate's hand. "I can do that." Her gaze shot to Fontaine. "At least I think I can."

"We'll get you set up in time to help Kate play the part."

Mrs. Brantley swept a hand over Kate's hair. "Although we're about the same height, I don't know how you'll get this blonde to look like me in time."

Royce chuckled. "I have access to a professional hairstylist and makeup artist. I think we can manage."

"Okay, then." Mrs. Brantley nodded. "I'm in."

Rex sighed. "Good, because I wasn't sure how I was going to remain standing much longer." He swayed, reached for the examination table, missed and would have fallen if Montana hadn't been there to catch him. "Thanks."

Montana looped Rex's arm over his shoulder. "Come on, I bet you could use a drink and a bed."

"Yes to both." Rex shot a narrow-eyed glance at his boss. "You aren't going anywhere, are you?"

Mrs. Brantley smiled. "No. Get some rest. I'll be here when you wake."

Montana helped Rex to the barracks-style room he would share with the SEALs and Royce's SOS agents.

Once he had the bodyguard settled, Montana glanced around at the men moving in and out, making use of the shower, one by one.

Sawyer settled in the bunk next to Montana's and linked his hands behind his head. He wore only a pair of boxers and his hair glistened with moisture. "Not the level of quality you had at the Jefferson, is it?"

"No." Montana dropped to the thin mattress and settled in, determined to catch some Zs so that he could be alert and ready to go for the next day's action.

"Kate seems to be a real ballbuster, doesn't she?" Sawyer said. "I can't believe she ran through the city streets barefooted and wearing nothing but a bathrobe. That's dedication, if you ask me."

"She's something, all right," Montana commented. Kate was as passionate about her job as she was in bed. And she was beautiful, toned and could kiss. Boy, could she kiss. But when she wrapped her legs around him and he sank inside her…

Montana swallowed hard to keep from groaning aloud.

"Yeah, you and Kate seem to make a good team." Sawyer yawned. "It doesn't hurt that she's got a body that doesn't quit."

Montana's fists clenched and a stab of something he could swear was jealousy knifed through his heart. If he didn't know Sawyer better, he'd be mad at his comment. Thankfully, Sawyer was in a relationship with a wonderful woman back in Mississippi. They had even started looking at engagement rings.

Forcing his hands to unclench, Montana lay still, staring up at the ceiling in the dim light filtering in from the bottom of the door to the hallway. He wondered what Kate was doing. Would she be asleep by now? Were her feet sore from running barefoot through the streets? Was she thinking about the shower in the Jefferson, like he was at that moment?

Montana rolled to his side and closed his eyes. He needed to sleep, but how could he when all he could think about was Kate's wet, naked body pressed against the shower stall?

After lying awake for another hour, listening to the other members of his team snoring or the bedsprings creaking, he gave up, got out of the bed and wandered out into the hall, hoping to find a kitchen and a glass of water. If he happened to run into Kate...well, he'd check and see how she was.

KATE HAD BEEN assigned to an office with a couch containing a hide-a-bed. After washing up and brushing her teeth with the toiletries Royce had provided, she'd removed the cushions from the couch and attempted to pull the bed out. No matter how many times she tried, it refused to budge.

After thirty minutes, a broken fingernail and a bruised ego, Kate gave up. One by one, she replaced the cushions, then lay on the couch, tucking the robe around her.

It wasn't the Jefferson with its ultrasoft mattress and goose-down comforter, but it would have to do for the night. Thoughts of the Jefferson set her on the path of remembering everything that had happened from the time she entered the room she'd shared with Montana to jumping out the window and racing after the bad guy.

No wonder her pulse still raced and she couldn't go to sleep. It had been an exciting evening. Even more exciting because of the shower she'd shared with Montana. Looking back, she should have felt a flash of guilt for making love with her partner, but it had felt so right she couldn't make herself feel wrong about it. She could still feel the cool tiles against her back and the way Montana had filled her so completely.

She rolled to her back and groaned. Making love to Montana was supposed to be a one-time thing, and then she was supposed to move on, get over him and banish him from her system.

"Yeah, how's that working out for you?" she whispered to the empty room. Sleep wasn't coming and she really needed rest to be on her toes the next day. Closing her eyes, she counted bullets in her head, then beer bottles and then sheep. Nothing helped.

Kate rolled off the couch and stood in her bathrobe, wondering if she could find a bottle of whiskey somewhere in the building. Maybe some of the fiery liquid would take the edge off her nerves and allow her to fall asleep.

With that goal in mind, she opened the office door, stepped out into the corridor and ran into a solid wall of muscle.

An arm clamped around her and a warm, buttery voice said, "You really should look before you leap."

Kate glanced up into the eyes of the man who'd made her night sleepless. Her pulse jacked up and pounded through her veins. "What are you doing awake?"

He chuckled. "I suspect the same thing you are. I was thinking about a certain shower in a certain hotel." He shook his head. "Once I went down that memory lane, I couldn't begin to go to sleep."

Kate considered denying that she had been consumed by the same thoughts and images. When she opened her mouth, she said, "Me, too." Then she did something she never thought she'd do in a bunker beneath the city. She turned toward her open door. "I don't suppose you can help me pull the bed out of this couch?"

His lips twitched. "Sure. But what's in it for me?"

"What's in it for you?" After a quick glance down the hallway, Kate took his hand, led him into the room and closed the door behind her. "You get to sleep on it."

Chapter Seven

Montana woke the next morning with Kate's warm body spooned into the curve of his own. For a long moment, he lay still, listening to the sound of her breathing and smelling the herbal scent of her shampoo.

He'd never stayed until morning in any woman's bed. In the middle of the night, the walls always seemed to close in on him. Lying awake with a naked female next to him would make him anxious to get up and leave, as though he would suffocate if he didn't get outside.

With Kate lying next to him in the basement bunker of a downtown DC building, Montana waited for the feeling of being strangled to force him out of the lumpy hide-a-bed and back to the makeshift barracks farther down the hallway. But that feeling never came. He'd slept better than he'd slept in a long time, with Kate nestled against him, her naked body warming his.

Once he'd pulled the bed out and they straightened the sheets, he'd lifted her into his arms and kissed her like he'd wanted to since they'd left the communications van. She'd responded with equal passion. From there, it was only natural for them to fall into the bed and make love until they had slaked their thirst for each other.

Making love with Kate had helped him to release the tension that had been building and keeping him awake. By the time they lay exhausted beside each other, Montana was able to fall into a deep and dreamless sleep. Without a window to let in sunlight, he didn't wake until he heard footsteps in the corridor outside the room.

A light tap on the door was followed by Tazer's voice. "McKenzie, are you awake?"

Kate stirred in his arms and stretched. "Yeah." She stared into Montana's eyes. "I'm awake." She ran her hand over his chest and downward.

"We need to get started. Can I come in?" The door handle wiggled.

Montana's heart leaped and he jerked to a sitting position.

Kate sat up as well, pulling the sheet up over her naked breasts.

Though the handle wiggled again, the door remained closed. "You'll have to unlock the door."

"Uh. Give me a minute to get dressed." Kate swung her legs over the side of the bed, fighting to free them from the sheet. "I can meet you in the conference room in five." Failing to get her legs free, she rose, wrapped mummy-style, and fell forward.

Montana dived across the bed, catching her before she performed a face-plant on the concrete flooring. Dragging her back into the bed, he swallowed hard on the laughter threatening to rumble up his chest.

"Don't you dare laugh," she whispered.

"You okay in there, McKenzie?"

"Yes, I am," Kate responded.

Montana nibbled at her earlobe. "Mmm, yes. You're more than okay."

"Shh." Kate touched a finger to his lips and tilted her head, listening for Tazer's footsteps. When the woman had left her post out in the hall, Kate relaxed and shook her head. "Thank you for locking the door last night. I completely forgot."

"I'm good for more than unfolding hide-a-beds." He kissed her neck again and trailed his lips lower to capture a rosy-tipped nipple between his teeth.

"Ouch." She shoved him away. "Those aren't for consumption." Kate smiled, cupped his face and pulled him up to kiss her properly. "Much as I'd love to stay in bed all day, we have a job to do. Can we take a rain check for after the show?"

Montana sighed. "You're right. I'm sure my team will be wondering where I've been, as well." He sat up, untangled her legs and waited for her to rise from the bed before he stood.

Kate stretched, her naked body a silhouette in the wedge of light shining from beneath the door. God, she was beautiful, her body perfect in every way.

Montana stepped up to her and pulled her against him, liking the feel of her skin against his.

Kate laced her hands behind his neck and pressed her breasts against his chest. "You know you tempt me, don't you?"

"No, I think it's the other way around. What say you and I call in sick and stay in bed all day?"

Kate nuzzled his neck. "Think the boss would understand?"

"Probably not."

"That's too bad." She ran her hand along his jawline and down to his chest. "Yeah, frogman, you tempt me more than I care to admit."

"Tonight?"

"You're on." She leaned up on her toes and pressed her lips to his in a brief, chaste kiss.

Montana captured her around her waist and held her there, his mouth crashing down on hers in a kiss he hoped was more than a promise of what they would have after the big gala. He'd count the minutes until that night. In the meantime, they had a job to do.

Kate stepped away, her lips bruised, her eyes shining and a rosy color blooming in her cheeks. "I have to go." She pulled on the only clothing she had, his pajama top and the bathrobe. "Give me a minute lead before you come out. The less everyone knows about our business, the better."

Montana's gut tightened. The sudden urge to tell the world that Kate McKenzie was his lover nearly burst from his chest. But she was right. If Fontaine knew they were getting too close, he might assign one of his teammates to play the part of Rex Masters.

Montana couldn't let that happen. He wanted to be there when the operation went down. Kate might be fully capable of helping herself out of a situation, but no one could undo the damage of a bomb. Having set his share of explosive devices, Montana knew what to look for and what kind of damage an explosion could cause.

Kate left, pulling the door closed behind her.

Montana folded the bed back into the couch, restoring the room into the office it was meant to be. Having burned the appropriate lead time, he edged the door open and glanced out into the corridor.

It was empty, but he could hear voices farther down the hallway. He ducked into the shower, rinsed off and toweled dry. Wrapping a towel around his waist, he hurried to the room he should have slept in the night before.

The guys were up and dressed, gearing up for the day ahead.

"Nice of you to join us," Rip said, his lips pulled back in a smirk.

"We were about to send out a search party to find you." Duff dragged back the slide on a .45 caliber pistol, checked the chamber and released the slide. "We're almost finished getting ready to go to the club. Tazer's been looking for you and Kate. Says she has a stylist waiting to start the transformation."

Sawyer passed Montana and clapped a

hand on his shoulder. "Better you than me. Couldn't stand to wear makeup."

"What do you think camouflage is?" Montana asked.

"It sure as hell isn't pink," Sawyer shot back.

The men all laughed out loud. After each had selected a gun and finished dressing in the uniforms of the yacht club employees, they filed past Montana.

The last one out was Duff. He clapped a hand on Montana's shoulder in turn. "Break a leg, bro."

"You, too. This will be one of those missions to tell your grandchildren about." Montana smiled. "When are you and Natalie going to tie the knot?"

Duff grinned. "I think I've found the right ring. When we get back to Mississippi, I'm going to take her out on the Pearl River and pop the question."

Montana stared at his friend. "The Pearl? Couldn't you take her on a beach vacation or at least to a nice restaurant to pop the question?"

"I want to take her fishing. If she still loves me after fighting the bugs and humidity, I'll know I've got a keeper."

"Seriously? The woman's already been

through hell in Cancun. You don't think that was enough?"

Duff's lips twisted. "You're right. I thought about taking her to a spa in Biloxi and signing up for one of those couples' massages. I could pop the question there."

"Now you're thinking straight." Montana shook his head. "Asking a girl on the Pearl is a surefire way to get her to not only say no, but *hell* no. What were you thinking?"

"That I like fishing?" Duff said. "And that I couldn't think of anyone else I'd like to go fishing with for the rest of my life."

"Save the fishing for a different occasion, like maybe your twenty-fifth anniversary."

Duff left Montana shaking his head.

If he were asking a woman to marry him, he'd take her somewhere with a beautiful sunset—a beach, the mountains, a cabin on a lake. He'd found that spot once in the mountains of Montana. That would be the ideal spot, if he could find it again.

He'd wait for the perfect moment, when the sky was at its most beautiful, then he'd get down on one knee and tell her she was the one person in the entire world he wanted to share that sunset with. He'd tell her that she was the woman he wanted to have children with, and have sitting next to him in a rocking chair on his front porch when they grew old, wrinkled and gray. Then he'd ask her to marry him and make him the happiest man in the world.

An image of Kate popped into his mind. Would a mountain lake appeal to a woman like her? Was she open to horseback riding and hiking into the backcountry to find the perfect location for a proposal? Montana had dreamed of eventually returning to his home state to live close to the mountains south of Bozeman. Any woman he hoped to marry would have to be open to such a move. Not all women liked living in such wide-open spaces, where the nearest shopping mall could be hundreds of miles away.

Not that he was thinking of popping the question anytime soon. He had to have a girlfriend first. Kate was just his partner for this operation. So they'd had sex. He hadn't assumed it committed them to a relationship. Kate was a very independent woman, burned by her former partner.

How any man could use her so ruthlessly, Montana couldn't imagine. Kate was beautiful, passionate and beyond fantastic in bed. His groin tightened. Drawing in a deep breath, he fought for control.

"You ready to get this party started?" a voice called out from behind him.

He spun, remembering at the last minute he wore only a towel around his middle.

Tazer stood in the doorway, a smile curling her lips. "Is that a banana under your towel or are you just happy to see me?"

Montana cursed.

"When you're dressed and ready to think with your mind, you can join us in the conference room. I'll tell them you'll be a few minutes."

"Thanks," he grumbled, and turned away, his cheeks burning.

KATE SAT FOR an hour with a stylist Royce had brought in. Leslie Saunders had been a makeup and hair artist in Hollywood before moving to Washington.

Tazer told Kate that Leslie had been blindfolded before they brought her to the secret site beneath the city, thus keeping their location safe. "Though I completely trust her. Leslie's saved my butt on more than one occasion."

Leslie wore a long, silk, royal blue oriental robe over a white camisole and white leggings. Her beautiful platinum-blond curls were pushed back behind her ears and secured with ornamental peacock-shaped combs. Her makeup matched her robe, framing her eyes with royal blue eye shadow and coal-black liner.

Kate felt like the ugly duckling next to her ethereal beauty.

Leslie fluffed Kate's hair, running her hands through the fine strands. "What are we doing here?"

Mica entered the room. "She needs to be the spitting image of me." Mrs. Brantley had applied her makeup as usual and arranged her hair as if she were attending the gala, the long, smooth strands neatly pinned into a subtle but elegant twist at the back of her head.

Leslie made several laps around Mica, studying her face and hair closely. Finally, she nodded. "I can do this." She opened the suitcase she'd brought and extracted bottles of liquid foundation, pallettes of contouring powder, blushes and eye shadows. Then she laid several tubes of eyeliner and mascara on the table, along with fake eyelashes and eyebrow pencils.

For the next thirty minutes, she worked on Kate's face like a painter on a blank canvas. When she was through with the makeup, she dug into her suitcase again and removed several dark wigs with long straight hair. One by one, she held them up to Mica's hair until she found one that most closely matched the color.

She slipped it over Kate's head and anchored it with pins in the back and at the sides. Then she applied a liquid to blend the cap with Kate's forehead. Once it was in place, she applied makeup to completely hide the edge, and swept the long hair up into a loose twist, allowing strands to fall around her face and neck.

Finally, Leslie called Mica over to stand beside Kate.

When she stepped back, Tazer gasped. Then a grin spread across her face. "Honey, I knew you were good, but wow. Just wow."

Kate had yet to see her reflection in the mirror. Mica looked the same as she had when she'd walked through the door an hour before, but Kate had no idea how closely they matched.

Leslie dug again in her suitcase, extracted a large mirror and handed it to her.

Mica bent and looked into the mirror at the same time as Kate.

Kate's breath caught in her throat and her heart skipped several beats. If she didn't know better, she'd bet the two women in the mirror were identical twins.

"Amazing," Mica said, her smile spreading across her face. "You're going to pull this off." Then her grin faded and she placed a hand on Kate's shoulder. "You could still back out of this. I don't want you hurt."

Kate patted the woman's hand. "I'm going. It's my choice. You lost your husband to this madman. I lost my mentor in the CIA. Becca lost her father. This has to stop."

"But I could go instead," Mica insisted.

"No. You're not trained to fight. I am. You said it yourself—I can pull this off. With you in my ear, I'll be you. No one will know the difference." Kate modified her voice, raising it to the pitch Mica used when she was worried or adamant. "I've been listening to you and watching your gestures." Kate waved her hand in the graceful style Mica displayed when she was more animated in her speech.

Tazer shook her head. "I can't tell the difference when you do that. It's uncanny."

Mica turned to Tazer. "But she shouldn't have to place herself in danger."

Kate faced Tazer and assumed the same stance and facial expression, as well as the way Mica held her arms and hands. "But she shouldn't have to place herself in danger," she mimicked, matching Mica's tones and inflections exactly.

Tazer laughed and clapped her hands. "Perfect." She glanced at her watch. "We don't have much time. We need to fit you for clothes and shoes. The outfits we chose yesterday are similar in taste and style as what Mrs. Brantley would wear. Since it's a gala, she wouldn't be expected to wear something she'd worn somewhere else. So new is good." Tazer opened a closet and pulled out the three outfits they'd purchased the previous day.

Mrs. Brantley studied the first one, then held up the second and smiled at the third. "I'd wear this to the gala."

The dress was a long, shimmering silver gown with narrow straps and a deep neckline, both in the front and back.

Tazer nodded. "I thought you might like that one. And it looks amazing on Kate."

"And I have the perfect necklace to go with it. I was planning on wearing it to the gala. I'll be right back." Mica left the room and returned in a minute carrying a sparkling diamond necklace, each gem exquisitely encased in white gold.

Kate shook her head, drawing the bathrobe around her body. "I can't wear that. It probably cost a fortune."

"Darling, if you don't wear it, they'll know

you're a fake for sure," Mrs. Brantley said. "Go on, get into the dress."

Kate dropped the robe and unbuttoned the pajama top, reluctant to let go of the one item of clothing she felt most comfortable in. That it was Montana's made it even harder to release.

Tazer held out the silver dress. She winked. "We're not prudes here, but if it helps, we can turn around." She started to do so.

"No, it's okay." Kate shrugged out of the pajama top and took the dress from Tazer. As she stepped into the garment, it slid across her legs and over her hips. She remembered liking the way it had felt in the dressing room at the shop.

Once Kate was zipped into the gown and the matching silver three-inch heels, Mrs. Brantley stepped behind her and placed the necklace around her neck.

Leslie handed her the mirror. "Honey, I couldn't have chosen better. You look fabulous."

Kate stared into the mirror. A different person stared back at her. If not for the gray-blue of her eyes, she wouldn't have recognized herself.

"Wait." Leslie dived into her bag again and came out with a package of colored contacts.

"You'll need the brown contacts or it'll be a dead giveaway. Attention to details pays off."

Leslie helped Kate insert the lenses.

She blinked several times before the contacts settled into place, at which point she could barely feel them.

"If you're ready, we need to get going." Tazer hooked her arm and led her toward the door.

"We have transportation that will take you to Mrs. Brantley's car. It's positioned at another hotel, where you're supposedly staying under another name," Tazer said. "Montana is waiting for you. The gala begins in less than an hour." She pressed a small radio earbud into Kate's hand. "Put this in your ear. It's your connection to Mrs. Brantley. And this rhinestone clip is just added bling to the dress. It contains a body cam. Mrs. B and the guys on the monitors will be able to see everything you see. Or at least everything you see at breast level." Tazer chuckled.

Kate's pulse picked up as she entered the corridor, her gaze searching for Montana. Her stomach clenched when she didn't find him.

Mrs. Brantley hurried alongside her. "You'll be deposited at the front of the yacht club onto a red carpet. The media will be there in full force. Remember to hold your head up and smile for the cameras. I'll be with you as soon as Lance gets me set up."

Kate smiled at Mica. "Thank you. I'll do my best to make you proud."

"Oh, and here." She pulled off her diamond wedding ring. "I wouldn't go anywhere without it." She held out her hand.

Kate reluctantly removed her fake wedding ring and handed it to Mica. "I want that back," she said, taking Mica's giant diamond ring.

Mica grinned. "Ditto." She curled her hand around the fake ring. "And remember, I wouldn't be there at all if not for the children. It's all about the children." She slowed to a stop as they neared the building's solid steel doors leading into the garage.

Royce's long dark limousine was parked on the other side. A man in a tuxedo stood beside it. When he turned, Kate had to look closely. The man looked like Rex, but when he smiled, she knew it was Montana. Hell, she'd seen him naked more than she'd seen him in clothes. The tuxedo made him appear broader and taller. "Larger than life" was the phrase that came to mind.

His eyes narrowed and he glanced from her to Tazer and back. "Kate?"

Adopting Mica's tone and persona, she answered, "I decided this event was too important to miss. Kate will be working with the men in the computer room." She ran her gaze from the top of his head to his shoes. "You'll do as a double for Rex. Are we ready?" She didn't wait for him to respond, but sailed around him to the limousine.

As she passed Montana she felt a sharp slap on her behind.

"Hey." She swung around and glared at him.

Tazer laughed. "Go get 'em, Kate. You'll do great."

Montana's smile widened. "I knew it was you all along."

"Yeah, well, you didn't have to slap me to prove it." Kate lowered herself into the backseat of the limo and swung her legs inside.

Montana closed the door, walked around to the other side and slid onto the seat beside her. "I like the real Kate better." His lips twitched, curling into a smile, and he reached out to take her hand in his.

The ride to the staging hotel took only ten minutes. The driver dropped them at the rear of the hotel garden. Montana led Kate through a gap in the fence and onto the path leading through a fragrant array of rosebushes. They emerged near a swimming pool and entered the back door of the grand hotel.

Taking their time, they ambled across the lobby and out the front entrance to Mica's waiting limousine.

Kate stared hard at the chauffeur. If she wasn't mistaken, it was Duff behind the cap and sunglasses. Feeling better and better about the situation, she settled into the backseat and glanced out the window at the buildings as they drove through the streets of downtown DC toward the Potomac River and the yacht club where the event was to take place.

For all she knew nothing would happen. On the flip side, if someone had managed to get a bomb inside the building, this could be the last time she saw sunshine. It could be her last day on earth. She wished she'd had time for one more stolen kiss. Instead, Kate reached for Montana's hand and squeezed it as the limousine pulled up in front of the club.

Chapter Eight

No matter how different she appeared in the wig, makeup and dress, the woman beside Montana was still Kate, through and through. She held herself like royalty and, if things went south, he had no doubt she'd come out kicking butt.

He reached into his inside pocket and pulled out a small gun with a thin Velcro strap. "I was going to give this to you for protection, but I can't imagine where you'd hide it. That dress fits you like a second skin."

"I'll find a place." She took the small device from him.

"You know how to use it?"

"I do." Kate lifted the hem of her gown, exposing a good portion of her smooth, sexy leg.

Montana's pulse quickened. What he wouldn't give to be back on that damned hide-a-bed, locked in an office in the basement of the SOS building, making love to Kate.

She strapped the gun to the inside of her thigh, above the slit in the dress, and slipped the skirt back in place.

Montana swallowed hard and patted the gun he had tucked in a shoulder holster inside his jacket. "Ready?"

She touched her finger to the earbud. "Ready?"

Mica must have answered with an affirmative, because Kate looked up at Montana and nodded.

He got out of the limousine and turned to hold the door for Kate. She was beautiful and a dead ringer for Mica Brantley. If the assassin who'd come for the widow last night found his way inside the yacht club today, he'd have to go through "Rex" to get to the fake Mica.

Using his body as a shield, Montana placed himself between her and the waiting crowd, cordoned off the red carpet by a line of velvet ropes. Members of the media crowded in, cameras flashing and shoving microphones in her face.

"Mrs. Brantley, this is your first time out in public since your husband's death. How does it feel?"

Kate gave a stiff smile. "No comment."

Montana firmly pushed the reporter and his microphone out of the way, allowing Kate to proceed toward the door.

A female reporter came at her from the other side. "Mrs. Brantley, your dress is stunning. Who are you wearing?"

Kate paused and answered the woman, stating a name Montana had never heard. She turned and posed for the cameraman, placing her hand on her hip, turning slightly to the side.

Montana almost laughed. He could swear the Kate he knew was more comfortable in jeans and a T-shirt. But this Kate handled the press like a pro. Like a celebrity. The woman had actress potential. He made a note to himself to ask if that's what they taught CIA agents in training. He choked on a laugh when he thought that while he'd lugged logs in the waves off San Diego, she'd studied clothing designers and posing for cameras. She'd probably flip him over her hip and smash his face into the concrete if he said anything along those lines.

Another reporter jammed his microphone in Kate's face. "Mica, now that your husband is dead, are you having an affair with your bodyguard?"

Her eyes narrowed slightly, but she didn't

respond to the question. Instead, she turned away from the man and climbed the steps toward the yacht club entrance.

Montana clenched his fists, holding on to his last nerve to keep from shoving his knuckles down the bastard's throat. Mica's husband was barely cold in the grave. How could the reporters be so heartless? Montana followed Kate's lead, refusing to rise to the rumormongers. He stayed close, keeping his body between her and the crowd.

Behind him, a reporter shouted above the melee, "Mrs. Brantley, did you murder your husband?"

Montana swung around, his gaze searching the throng for the man who'd had the audacity to accuse Mrs. Brantley of killing her husband.

Kate's hand on his arm stopped him from charging down the steps to crush the monster.

"He's not worth it," she said. "Let's do this."

Montana ground his teeth and shot a killing glare at the media, then turned on his heel, placed his hand at the small of Kate's back and followed her into the club.

Inside, the crowd wasn't nearly as pressing or overwhelming, but there were a lot of people milling about, dressed in their finest, strutting around like a flock of peacocks. Or was it a gaggle of peacocks, he wondered. No, it was something stranger… An ostentation!

Montana shook his head. Ostentatious was more like it. This group of men and women spent more on what they were wearing than most people earned in a month. All for a party. If they put all that money in with the amount they donated to the children's hospital, they'd amass a significantly greater amount for the cause.

"Mica, darling." A gray-haired woman in a dark blue dress rushed forward and would have engulfed her in a hug if Montana hadn't seen her coming and stepped between them at the last moment.

Kate placed a hand on his arm. "Rex, please. This is Mrs. Martin. One of our most generous patrons. I'm sure she's not here to harm me."

"Oh, certainly not," the woman said. "I love Mica like a daughter."

Montana eased out of the way, and the older woman hugged Kate so tightly, she grimaced.

"I was so sad to hear about Trevor. Such a good man. And he was so young."

"Thank you, Mrs. Martin."

"Are you doing well?" She stared into

Kate's face. "You look a little peaked. You should go someplace where you can get some sun. Fresh air and sunshine helps when you lose a loved one."

Kate smiled. "I'll consider your advice when I plan my next trip."

Mrs. Martin patted her arm. "Please, if you need a place to stay while you're in the city, consider staying with me, not some cold, impersonal hotel. You're always welcome."

"Thank you, Mrs. Martin. You're too kind."

Mrs. Martin's attention darted to the left. "Oh, look. There's Janine Anderson. I must say hello. Will you be all right on your own?"

Kate nodded. "I have Rex to keep me company."

The older woman glanced at Montana as if noticing him for the first time. "Oh, yes. Of course you do. He is quite handsome. I think every woman should have a handsome bodyguard to keep her company in these dangerous times. Excuse me, I have to catch Mrs. Anderson." Mrs. Martin hurried away.

"One acquaintance down, only a hundred to go," Montana whispered.

"Thank goodness for technology," Kate whispered back. She smiled as another of

Mica's friends approached her and engaged her in conversation.

Kate handled each person with care and dignity, much like Mrs. Brantley would have had she been there. With the woman feeding information into her ear, Kate was able to ask about one couple's daughter in college, another man's sickly mother and an elderly woman's son in the army.

Montana kept a close watch on Kate and looked around the crowded ballroom, searching for anyone who seemed out of place, angry or nervous. The security at the entrance was tight, but anyone who wanted to get into the yacht club badly enough would find a way.

On several occasions, he spotted his teammates, weaving in and out among the guests, carrying trays of hors d'oeuvres or glasses of champagne. Fontaine and Tazer appeared at the entrance as guests.

Tazer wore a long black gown, her blond hair piled high on her head, and long sparkling earrings hanging from her earlobes. Fontaine wore a black tuxedo that made his shock of white hair look even more prestigious. The man knew how to blend in to any crowd of people.

When the SOS leader glanced their direction, he gave the slightest dip of his head in acknowledgment. With six SEALs, two SOS agents and one CIA undercover operative at the gala, if something were to happen, they'd have an excellent chance of either stopping it or catching whoever initiated the fight.

Fontaine reported that the dogs hadn't come across anything that smelled even remotely like explosives. Not only had the team been through the building multiple times, they'd been at the loading dock for each delivery that day, up until the gala actually started.

Metal detectors had been set up at the entry points to scan for guns and weapons. All the right precautions had been taken. Still, Montana had a gut feeling something would happen that night. He'd been in enough firefights to trust his gut. He stuck to Kate throughout the evening. When it came time for her to address the gathering and laud the virtues of contributing to the children's hospital, he wasn't happy with how exposed she'd be on the stage.

As she started to climb the steps, he was right behind her.

Kate stopped halfway up and placed a hand on his chest. "I can handle this."

"No one can handle a bullet through the heart."

"I'll stay behind the podium," she said.

"It's made of wood. It'll only slow the bullet."

"Please." Kate smiled. "I'm here for the children."

"I'm here to make sure you live to *have* children," he insisted.

She stared into his eyes for a long moment. He held her brown-eyed gaze, refusing to back down, wishing he could see her gray eyes through the contact lenses.

"Okay." She straightened and continued upward. "But try not to look so big and intimidating. We want the people to donate, not run screaming."

Montana chuckled and fought the urge to slap her bottom. He followed her to the podium, standing back a few steps, putting on a poker face as he scanned the crowd, searching for anyone who looked like he might pull a gun and start firing.

Kate welcomed the guests with a smile and spoke eloquently the words Mrs. Brantley had prepared for her speech.

Montana half listened, balancing on the balls of his feet, ready to launch himself in front of Kate at any moment.

SO FAR, THE event was going as planned, with no surprises and no attacks. Kate relaxed in her role, reading the speech Mrs. Brantley had given her before she'd left for the gala.

She'd been amazed at the statistics Mrs. B had compiled about all the children the hospital had helped at no cost to the families, and all the children who were still alive due to the care they'd received. At the conclusion of the speech, she called for people to open their hearts and wallets. She stepped back, thankful she hadn't been interrupted by gunfire and was able to do the speech justice for Mrs. Brantley.

A commotion at the side of the stage caught her attention. Montana stepped forward, using his body as a shield for hers.

Kate leaned around Montana to find a woman herding a group of twenty or more children in choir robes up onto the stage.

"They brought children to the gala?" she said softly. "Who authorized that?"

Mrs. Brantley's laughter filled Kate's ear. "They always have a children's choir sing at the gala. It makes the guests more aware of how important it is to protect them and help them when they are sick."

"But they're children," Kate said. "What if something happens?"

Mrs. Brantley didn't respond right away. "I

didn't think about that. Really, I'd forgotten about the choir altogether."

Kate glanced at Montana. "We have to get them out of here."

The woman in charge of the choir smiled at Kate and proceeded to organize the children on the stage.

Kate gritted her teeth, her gaze sweeping the room as she prayed that whoever might attack her or anyone else present would consider waiting until the children sang their song and left the club.

All through the three verses of "Hallelujah," Kate worried. They finally finished, and the woman herded them down the steps and out of the club.

Kate released the breath she'd held. With her speech obligation complete, she had no reason to remain at the club. She descended the stairs with Montana close behind. No bullets flew, no bombs went off. If they were lucky, the entire gala, the coordinates and date would be a nonevent.

"Ah, Mrs. Brantley." A man with graying hair and a slight paunch approached her, smiling. "Thank you for a moving speech. Your husband would have been so proud."

Montana moved closer, his eyes narrowing.

"This man is Nigel Carruthers," Mica said

into Kate's ear. "He's a dear friend of Trevor's. They've known each other since they were roommates at Harvard. I usually hug him."

"Nigel. It's so good to see you." Kate hugged the man and then stood back, smiling. "Thank you for the kind words."

"I miss playing golf with Trevor. Just the other day, I walked by my clubs and wished I could have given him a call to go out and hit a few balls." The man sighed. "A shame to lose such a talented man."

Kate nodded and waited for Mrs. Brantley to feed her more information. For a long moment, she didn't speak. "My husband loved playing golf, but he wasn't very good at it. He did it to get outside in the fresh air more than anything. Nigel always won."

"Trevor would have loved to get out in this wonderful weather we're having lately," Kate said.

Carruthers nodded. "Although he'd been pretty busy with his latest projects, he made time to play a few rounds with me before he passed." The older man looked up and gave her a sad smile. "I imagine if he'd known he wouldn't be around much longer, he might have spent more time with his family. Emily might not have gone to New York and been abducted."

Mrs. Brantley gasped. "Trevor loved us more than himself. He wouldn't have committed so much time to his project had he not considered it important. He was devastated when Emily went missing. He dropped everything to search for her."

Kate stared at the man in front of her, wanting to kick him for being so inconsiderate. He obviously hadn't known the Brantleys as well as he thought.

"Family is everything," Carruthers continued. "You should know that now more than ever, right, Mica?"

"I don't know why Nigel is being so hurtful. He should know how hard it is for me. Nigel lost his brother several years ago in an embassy bombing. I remember how distraught he was. Trevor was there for him, helping him through the difficulty of having his brother's body returned to the States, and arranging for his funeral."

"Nigel, we both miss Trevor," Kate said, searching for words to say to the man who'd just insulted a grieving widow.

Carruthers grabbed her arm and squeezed hard enough to hurt her. "Trevor didn't tell you what he was working on, did he?"

"No, he didn't," Mrs. Brantley said.

"No," Kate repeated, twisting her arm in an attempt to free it from the man's grip.

Montana grabbed Carruthers's wrist and pulled it free of Kate's arm. "Please, don't touch Mrs. Brantley."

Carruthers glared at Montana and then turned to Kate. "I just wonder if he thought through whatever it was that he was doing and the implications it had on his family. If he had, would he have considered it worth it?" Carruthers stepped away from Kate and Montana, spun on his heels and left the ballroom.

"What the hell was that all about?" Montana stared at the man's retreating figure.

Kate rubbed her arm where a bruise was beginning to darken her skin. "I don't know. We need to check him out. See what his story is."

"He's been a bitter man since his brother's death," Mrs. B said. "Losing someone tends to change the ones left behind."

Kate could imagine. But that didn't give Carruthers the right to be so aggressive.

A band started playing in the far corner of the ballroom, the sound drowning out conversation.

If Kate could, she would have left at that moment. Her feet hurt, she was tired of pretending to be who she wasn't and her face itched from all the makeup.

But they were there in case something happened. At this point, it didn't appear as though it ever would.

A scream ripped through the air, the only sound that could be heard over the band being amplified through the speaker system.

One scream led to another, and the entire roomful of people surged toward the exit.

Kate craned her neck to see over the tops of people's heads. As the crowd thinned, she caught a glimpse of a group of people gathered in a circle, looking at something on the floor.

Kate pushed through the men and women heading for the door to get to the circle. Then she elbowed her way in to find a man lying on the polished marble tiles, his face gray, his eyes bulging and foam dripping from his mouth.

Well, damn. Even with all the precautions they'd taken, they hadn't been able to stop someone from taking yet another life. No guns or bombs were used to eliminate the subject. Nothing so barbaric. No. This time the attack had been with what appeared to be poison.

Chapter Nine

Police stopped everyone from leaving the yacht club. An ambulance arrived within five minutes, and emergency medical technicians were on the scene so fast Montana suspected Royce had had them on standby.

Nothing they did helped the guy who'd been poisoned. Apparently the toxin used was fast-acting and permanent. Montana's fists clenched and he hovered near Kate, refusing to budge from her side. His team circled the throng, watching closely, ready to spring into action.

Royce conferred with the police and EMTs, but didn't make contact with any of the others. They'd have time back at the SOS alternate site to put their heads together, review the videos and discover where their logic had gone wrong.

Montana couldn't wait to get Kate out of

the ballroom. He didn't feel that she was any safer with a roomful of police. If anything, the chaos of adding more people to the mix only made him more anxious to get her to safety.

"Stop worrying. I wasn't the one who was poisoned." She pushed him to the side. "And you can quit blocking my view. You're making me crazy."

He'd pretty much backed her into a corner and stood in front of her. It was the only way he could be certain no one would get a shot at her while attention was on the guy who'd been poisoned.

"Now would be the time to make another attempt," Montana said.

"Move." She shoved him to the side and stared at the first responders, firefighters and police. "What the hell? What's wrong with Royce?"

Montana's gaze shot to the last place he'd seen Fontaine and Tazer, standing beside the man in charge of the scene.

Fontaine was leaning heavily on Tazer, his face pale.

Tazer shouted for help.

EMTs converged on Fontaine and eased him onto a gurney. The emergency crew went to work stabilizing the leader of the SOS.

Kate started forward.

Montana's hand shot out, grabbing her arm. "We're not supposed to know him."

"But he's our friend. He's one of the team."

"What can you do to help?" Montana reasoned.

"I don't know. But I can't just stand here."

"What's going on?" Duff's voice sounded in Montana's ear.

"Fontaine is down," he responded. "Could be the same problem as the first victim."

Duff cursed. "Give me bullets and mortars any day. Poisoning guests is pure evil."

"Someone needs to go with Fontaine."

"Sawyer's on the outside of the building. He can go with Fontaine and Tazer to the hospital. In the meantime, you need to get Mrs. Brantley out."

Montana glanced toward the main exit, swarmed by at least a dozen police officers. "Can't get past the cops."

"Head toward the kitchen. There's a back exit they haven't completely closed off yet. We can create a distraction while you slip out."

Montana hooked Kate's arm. "Time to go."

"But what about Royce?" Kate dug in her heels and pulled against his grip on her arm. "What happened to *no man left behind*?"

"Tazer has his back. Sawyer is one of the security guards on the outside. He'll go with them to the hospital. Royce isn't being left behind. We can't do as much good as the doctors at the hospital can. Hopefully, he didn't get a full dose of whatever killed victim number one."

Kate allowed Montana to escort her through the crowd to the back of the ballroom and through a swinging door into the kitchen.

The state crime lab was already at work collecting evidence from the trays of food and champagne flutes. The caterers were being questioned and names were recorded.

"Never mind the kitchen," Duff's voice said from behind them. "Follow me."

He led them down a hallway lined with doors bearing gold nameplates. At the end of the hallway was another door labeled Yacht Shop.

Duff pulled a small metal file from his pocket, slid it into the keyhole and wiggled it several times.

Montana watched behind them, sure a police officer would find the hallway and haul them back inside the ballroom for questioning.

A metal click sounded and Duff chuckled.

"Works every time." He opened the door and led the way into the shop.

Kate went next and Montana brought up the rear, closed the door behind them and twisted the lock.

Duff weaved through the racks of windbreakers, hats and life vests to the opposite end of the shop, where another door led to the dock outside.

He paused, his gaze fixed to a plastic box on the wall with a keypad. "Looks like a security system. Be prepared to run if we trigger it."

"Maybe we should go back inside and wait our turn to be questioned," Kate said. "I'd hate for Mrs. Brantley to have to explain why she bypassed investigation protocol to leave the premises of the yacht club."

A loud click sounded.

Duff smiled, tapped his ear and said, "Thanks, Geek. We owe you." He opened the door. "I don't know how he does it, but that man is a magician. And he said he could substitute footage on the video feed without leaving a trace." He waved Kate through. "Let's get you out of here."

Kate stepped through the door and out onto the wooden planks of the dock. A maze of platforms led away from the club into the marina, where dozens of yachts were moored.

Montana slipped his arm around Kate's waist and helped her navigate the boards to keep her heels from getting caught in the gaps. "We can't really go around to the front of the building. How do you propose to get back to SOS headquarters?"

Duff smiled. "Royce had that covered, as well." He strode toward an intersection of the wooden walkway and turned left. Then he dropped out of sight.

Kate gasped and hurried toward the point where he'd vanished.

Montana followed. Below the decking was a small skiff tied to a ladder.

Duff grinned up at them. "Get in. We'll take this to the park on the Potomac that's only two blocks from our destination."

Kate removed her shoes and dropped them into the bottom of the boat. Then she lifted the hem of her dress and draped it over her arm.

"Tell you what. Let me go first," Montana said. "If you have any troubles, I can catch you."

"Why not let Duff?" she asked.

Montana shook his head. "I'd rather be the one. I'm your bodyguard, not Duff."

Kate's lips quirked upward. "You just don't want him ogling my behind."

Montana nodded, keeping his expression serious. "There is that."

She shook her head and moved to the side. "After you."

He hurried to get several rungs down the ladder before he paused. "Now you."

Kate eased her foot onto the first one and started down.

Montana waited for her to lower herself into the circle of his arms, and together they descended into the small skiff.

Duff sat at the tiller, his hand on the motor's start switch. "As soon as you take a seat, we'll get going."

Once Kate's feet touched the bottom of the boat, Montana took her hand and helped her to sit on one of the benches.

Montana took his seat.

Duff started the engine and eased the small craft out of the marina and into the main channel of the Potomac River. Though the boat wasn't equipped with the required lights for night boating, the lights from the city were sufficient to navigate the river in that area.

Montana prayed they'd make it to the park without being pulled over by the river police and ticketed for boating without the proper equipment. If they were discovered, they might also be arrested for leaving a crime scene without permission.

Past caring, Montana stared at the smooth water ahead. Light from the buildings on both sides of the channel outshone the stars above. Navigating didn't require a light for them to see. The legally required lights were more to make the boat visible to others on the water, to avoid collisions.

"Anything on Fontaine?" Duff said behind them.

Montana glanced over his shoulder at his teammate in the rear.

Kate turned in her seat and looked, as well.

Duff cupped a hand over his ear, his eyes narrowed. Then he nodded. "On our way to the pickup location. Roger. Out."

He glanced up and shook his head. "Nothing yet. Fontaine made it to the hospital and was taken straight back. Tazer is with him."

Montana returned his attention to the river in front of them, his gaze trained on the banks, searching for any signs of movement.

They reached the park and slid up on the shore. Montana jumped out and reached for Kate's hand.

She stepped off the front of the boat, slipped on the muddy bank and fell into his arms.

He held her close, glad to have the excuse for however short the time. Even before the death in the ballroom, he'd been tense, worried and waiting for something to happen. He didn't like that Kate was the decoy, but he wasn't calling the shots for her. If she hadn't wanted to take on the assignment, she would have voiced her opinion. The woman had a mind and heart of her own.

He admired that about her. At the same time, he didn't want her heart to be pierced by a bullet or stopped by poison in her bloodstream.

"You might want these." Duff held out Kate's heels.

Kate took them, but didn't move out of Montana's arms. A shiver rippled through her.

The warm spring air had turned chilly after the sun had set. Montana shrugged out of his tuxedo jacket and wrapped the garment around her shoulders.

She smiled up at him. "Thank you."

He frowned. "You should have said something on the boat."

"I'm okay."

Headlights flashed above in the park.

"That will be our transportation." Duff led the way up the bank and past picnic tables, to where Fontaine's limousine was waiting for them.

A dark-haired man got out and held out his hand. "Glad to see you made it out of the circus. I'm Sam Russell, SOS. Royce had me waiting on standby. I would have been at the gala, but I just got back in town this afternoon from another assignment."

Duff and Montana shook hands with Sam.

Kate stepped up to him and held out her hand. "Nice to meet you, Sam."

"Wow," he said. "I've seen Leslie's work before, but this is amazing. I ran into Mica Brantley at HQ. You look exactly like her."

Kate nodded. "Leslie gave up her career in Hollywood too soon."

"To our benefit," Sam added. He held open the door for her.

Kate slid in.

Montana got in beside her.

"I'll ride up front with Sam," Duff said.

Sam drove the limousine out of the park and onto the main road leading back into the city.

Beside Montana, Kate shivered and hunkered deeper into his jacket.

He draped his arm over her shoulders. “Better?”

“Yes. These dresses weren’t meant for running around outside in fifty-degree temperatures.”

“No, they weren’t.” Montana pulled her closer.

“Do you think the man who was poisoned was a random killing?” she asked.

“Not at all. Hopefully, by the time we get back to headquarters, Geek and Lance will have the victim’s identity. I would bet he ties into the other killings in some way.”

“Yeah, but we have yet to figure out the connection between all those who’ve been targeted thus far.” She leaned into him. “Why Trevor Brantley? Better still, why his daughter?” Kate shook her head. “I can understand wanting to take Mica out, since she’s on a relentless hunt to find the ones responsible. But why Emily Brantley?”

“I don’t know. Something Carruthers said tonight made me wonder. What project was Brantley working on? Was it what made him and his family a target?”

“It’s worth digging into. Maybe Mrs. Brantley can shed some light on that.”

"She said her husband had contacts that led her to the human trafficking chain in Cancun. Fontaine said he searched down that rabbit hole and came to a dead end. Mica's contacts were either killed or disappeared off the radar."

The limousine slammed to a halt, throwing Kate and Montana forward, tumbling across the floor.

No sooner had Montana righted himself than he lurched sideways, when the vehicle swerved.

"Hold on," Sam said. "We have two SUVs trying to hem us in."

Montana dived for the seat, strapped his seat belt and then reached for Kate. He grabbed her hand and yanked her up against his body as another vehicle rammed into them.

Refusing to let go, he held on as they rocked to the side, the SOS vehicle's left side leaving the ground, then crashing back down on all four wheels.

Sam gunned the accelerator, cut hard to the right, jumped the curb and drove down the sidewalk for several yards before bumping back onto pavement.

Montana pushed Kate into the seat beside him. Kate hiked her dress up, planted her knees in the seat and pulled her tiny gun from the strap around her thigh. Then she rolled down the window and leaned out.

"What the hell are you doing?" Montana shouted.

"Fighting back," she said.

Montana released his seat belt, pulled his pistol from his shoulder holster and leaned out his side of the vehicle.

One SUV flanked the limousine on the left. The other followed so closely behind, he could hit—

"Get down!" Montana grabbed a handful of her dress and pulled her back on the seat.

The SUV behind them rammed into their rear, while the other swerved to the left and raced up along the driver's side.

Kate rolled up on her knees, waited until the driver of the vehicle was in range and then fired into the tinted passenger-side window.

The driver jerked away and then came back.

Kate recoiled just in time.

The SUV rammed into the side of the limousine.

Kate tumbled across the floor.

As Montana bent forward to grab her hand, the trailing SUV clipped the corner of the limousine's left rear bumper.

The SOS vehicle spun to the right, ran over the curb and slammed into a covered bus stop.

Sam shifted and tried to back up, but the SUV that had been following pulled to a stop behind them, blocking that route of escape. The one that had blown past them was backing toward them at a fast clip, with no sign of slowing.

"Stay down," Montana said. He threw open his door, rolled out onto the ground and away from the limo as the second SUV backed into them.

Rage drove him to his feet, his gun drawn. He hunkered low behind the limousine, rounded the driver's side of the SUV and fired point-blank into the tinted window.

The glass shattered and Montana could see inside. He'd hit the passenger, but the driver was seated so far back, he'd only been grazed. He stomped his foot on the accelerator, sending the SUV leaping forward.

Montana fired into the vehicle, then leaped back to avoid having his feet run over.

The SUV that had backed into the limousine spun tires in an attempt to shoot forward. The back window slid down.

Montana didn't wait for it to make it all the way down before he fired his last five bullets into the vehicle. He released the clip and reached into his pocket for another, realizing at the last moment he didn't have one.

He was a sitting duck with no ammo. This couldn't end well.

WHEN THE LIMOUSINE had been hit by the backing vehicle, Kate had been slung sideways, slamming against a padded wall, her tiny pistol knocked from her grip. The *bang, bang, bang* sound of gunfire made her scramble to find the gun. Once she had it in her hand, she sat up, rolled over and out the open door Montana had escaped through.

Montana stood at the rear of the vehicle, firing at an SUV driving away from the fray.

The flash of relief Kate felt was short-lived when a man popped up over the top of the other SUV and fired at Montana.

Montana flung himself to the ground and rolled toward the limousine.

Kate couldn't see him, but was almost positive he wasn't behind any cover, which meant he was exposed to the man's gunfire.

Her heart leaped into her throat. She turned her little pistol toward the shooter and fired. The man ducked down and the SUV jerked forward, the tires smoking against the pavement.

Kate fired again, aiming for the driver. The

bullet hit the rear windshield, but the vehicle kept going.

Duff staggered out of the limousine, blood dripping down his face from a cut on his forehead. "Are you all right?"

Kate nodded. "But I'm not so sure about Montana."

"I'm okay," Montana called out from the other side of the vehicle. "Thanks to whoever was shooting there at the end." He stood and glanced from Kate to Duff.

Duff held up his hands. "It wasn't me. You can thank Kate." He pressed his fingers to his injured forehead. "We need to get the limousine free of the bus stop."

"What about Sam?"

"He's okay, just shaken up." Duff handed his gun to Kate. "You cover while we push." He waved to Montana. "Come on. We don't have time to answer a bunch of questions. We need to get to headquarters."

Kate stood guard, watching for a return of the two SUVs, the heavier 9 mm pistol fitting nicely in her palm. She'd shoot to kill if either of the vehicles reappeared.

Montana and Duff leveraged themselves between the front of the limousine and the bus stop's metal pole and pushed.

Sam had the vehicle in Reverse, his foot on the accelerator. At first the tires only spun.

Montana bounced the front of the hood and eventually whatever was holding the limousine worked loose.

Sam blasted backward, off the sidewalk and back onto the street.

Duff, Montana and Kate dived into the limousine, and Sam drove away from the bent pole of the bus stop.

Kate would have felt guilty about leaving it a mess if she didn't have a raging headache and bruises all over her body from being bounced around the interior of the limousine like a ball in a pinball machine.

"How did they find us?" she asked, as soon as the doors closed. "We could have been anywhere in the city. How did they know we would be at that exact place, at that exact time?"

In the front of the vehicle, Sam shook his head. "I was careful to keep an eye on the rearview mirror. I'm ninety-nine percent positive they didn't follow me to the pickup location. If they had, you'd think they would have attacked sooner."

Kate didn't believe the attackers had accidentally found them driving on the streets of the nation's capital. The SOS vehicle was as nondescript as a limousine could be, and looked like any one of hundreds that moved about the city at any time of the day, carrying politicians, lobbyists and various celebrities trying to be seen or heard supporting their pet causes. And Royce seemed like too much of a professional to leave the same license plate on his car all the time. He'd have it changed each time he made use of the company vehicle.

"Could the limousine be tagged with a tracking device?" Kate asked.

"We swept it before I left HQ," Sam said. "Geek is top-notch at encryption. Since we had the takeover last year, Geek's made it his mission to lock down access. No one can get into our system but him, Lance and Royce."

"Could one of us be tagged?" Montana asked.

Kate glanced down at her dress. "If I've been tagged, I don't know where they would have hidden it." She tugged at the bodice of her gown. "I barely have room in this dress for me."

Montana reached for his tuxedo jacket, which had ended up on the floor of the limousine.

He checked every pocket, carefully feeling for anything out of the ordinary, no matter how small. When he came up empty, he handed the jacket to Kate.

She repeated the search, while Montana checked his trouser pockets.

He dug deeply into each, checking every corner. Then he went still and his lips thinned into a straight line. “Son of a bitch.”

Montana pulled his hand out of his pocket and held up a tiny metal disk the size of a watch battery.

Chapter Ten

"You found it?" Duff turned and stared over the back of the seat.

Kate took the device from Montana's hand. "Someone probably slipped it into your pocket in the crush of guests at the club."

"We need to ditch it before those goons circle back for round two of bumper cars," Sam said.

Kate lowered the window on the undamaged side of the limousine and cocked her arm.

Montana grabbed her wrist before she could throw the disk into the street. "Wait." He nodded toward the front windshield.

A street cleaning machine moved slowly ahead of them, brushes spinning in an effort to keep the city streets trash free.

"Switch places," Montana said.

Kate slid over his lap.

He caught her hips as she did so, squeezed gently and then let her continue to the other side of the vehicle. As they pulled up behind the street cleaner, Sam slowed to match the big machine's crawl. Montana jumped out of the moving limousine, ran up to the back of the cleaner and planted the tracker.

He returned to the limo in a matter of seconds and hopped into the backseat.

Sam drove around the cleaner and sped away, performing a number of switchbacks through the streets until they were confident they hadn't been followed.

Forty-five minutes after they'd left the yacht club, they pulled through the overhead door of the SOS building and parked in the underground garage.

Quentin, Hunter and Rip emerged from the building and surrounded the car.

"We were about to send out the posse to find you," Hunter said. "Why did you turn off your radios?"

Montana, Duff and Kate raised their hands to their ears.

"We must have dropped them in the crashes," Duff said. "No matter, we're here now. What's the news on Fontaine?"

"Last we heard, he was still in the ER," Quentin said. "Sawyer hasn't seen or heard from Tazer to know if Fontaine made it through."

Rip stepped forward and looked at the cut on Duff's forehead. "Looks like you were in a fight. What happened?"

"We'll explain inside," Duff said.

Montana pushed past the others, pulling Kate with him. "We want to know who the victim is and see for ourselves who planted the poison."

Hunter fell in step behind them. "Lance and Geek are combing through the video footage of the party, trying to determine the point at which the victim and Fontaine were poisoned."

Each person took a moment to glance into the security camera. After all of them had done this, the door lock clicked and Hunter pushed through. By the time they'd reached the computer room, Kate's head was throbbing. She could barely wait to trade the dress for a long, soft T-shirt. "I'll be right back." She hurried to the infirmary, riffled through the stores of over-the-counter drugs for ibuprofen and downed two with a bottle of water.

By the time she returned to the computer room, Lance and Geek had their heads together, staring at a screen depicting the ballroom as people began to filter in.

Slowly advancing the images, they pored over the forty-five minutes before Kate's speech.

Montana scanned the crowd, looking for the man who'd died that night.

Geek pointed at the monitor. "There's Royce and Tazer, entering the ballroom."

"Look behind them." Montana leaned forward, excitement rippling through him. "See the two men following them?"

Kate leaned over Lance's shoulder. "Is that the dead guy? The one on the left?"

Montana nodded. "The guy on the floor had on a dark purple cummerbund."

"So does he," Kate whispered. "Dark hair, longish sideburns. It has to be him." She turned to Geek. "Any idea who that might be?"

"You're kidding, right?" Geek glanced up at Kate and Montana. "That's the guy who died tonight?" He shook his head and turned to another keyboard and monitor, where he clicked several keys, entered some data and then waited. Images popped up of the man shaking hands with the vice president of the United States, with the secretary of state and with a prominent member of the United Nations. And there he was sitting with the president in the Oval Office.

"Who is he?"

"Tarek Abusaid, the Syrian ambassador, here to ask the president for assistance in peace negotiations between his country and the Islamic State fighters attempting to completely overthrow the Syrian government."

"What the hell was he doing at the yacht club gala?" Montana asked.

Geek clicked on an image of Abusaid and the man who also appeared in the gala video. "He's a personal friend and distant cousin of the man with whom he arrived, Nizar Sayid, a naturalized US citizen born in Syria, raised in Massachusetts. Their mothers are cousins. Says here that Sayid is a pediatric oncologist at the children's hospital."

"Are we dealing with Islamic terrorists?" Sam asked.

Geek shook his head. "Not all of the people who've died or have disappeared seem to have a connection to each other or Abusaid."

Lance stood and walked to a large whiteboard with a long timeline sketched across it. He drew a short, perpendicular line on it, assigned the current date and Abusaid's name. On another portion of the board, all the names were written, with lines drawn between them and notes that had been jotted.

Montana crossed to the board and stared at the drawing.

"From what Rand Houston told us when we were in Cancun, he was working with the two CIA agents on the human trafficking issues."

Kate pointed at Rand Houston's name and followed the line connecting him to Marcus Smith. "He worked with Marcus Smith and Oscar Melton. My bosses." She pointed at Marcus's name. "Becca's father mailed her the disk with the dates and coordinates. He thought it important enough to mail it versus hand it to her in person."

Montana touched his finger to the board where Becca's name had been written. "Becca followed a lead about a certain mercenary heading to Cancun. Through her contacts, she came to believe the mercenary was the man who'd killed her father."

Quentin joined them at the board. "Mica Brantley showed up in Cancun following her lead about an auction selling women, in her attempt to find her stepdaughter, Emily." He pointed to Emily's name. "Trevor Brantley's daughter."

"Trevor," Kate added, "according to Nigel Carruthers, the man we met tonight, was working on a special project that was taking him away from spending time with his beloved family."

"Here's something interesting we learned today," Geek said. "Carmelo DeVita, the Mexican drug lord you ran into in Mexico, is involved in more than just drugs and selling women. We knew he sold arms as well, but we learned to whom today."

Montana turned toward Geek. "Who?"

Geek glanced over his shoulder. "Syrian rebels. ISIS. The Islamic State, who are terrorizing Syria, Iraq, France, England, Belgium, and who knows where they'll strike next."

"And the Syrian ambassador was murdered tonight." Kate lifted one of the dry-erase markers, wrote "Tarek Abusaid" on the board and then drew a line between Carmelo DeVita and the Syrian ambassador. "There's the Syrian connection here. Do you suppose they used the money from the sales of the women to fund the guns and fighting?"

Montana nodded. "And what better way to stir up more trouble in Syria than to kill the ambassador who had come to talk peace?"

"What do you want to bet there's a connection between Trevor Brantley, the CIA agents and the gunrunning to Syria?"

Kate looked at the board. "Who's Cassandra Teirney?"

"She was heavily involved in kidnapping the women," Duff said.

"Cassandra is just one of her many names," Geek said, without looking away from the monitor. "She spent time in prison for identity theft. She's been seen in and around DC. Our sources think she bases out of this area and reports to someone. She's smart, but not necessarily smart enough to pull off something as big as murdering a dozen people and not leaving a crumb for us to—" Geek cursed. "Speak of the devil, check this out."

Montana crossed to the bank of monitors and followed the cursor Geek was using to point to a woman in the crowded ballroom.

He enlarged the woman's face, made a copy of it and dropped it into another program. "If it's who I think it is, we should have a hit in five, four, three—" He pointed to the monitor as a woman dressed in prison orange came up next to the face he'd pulled from the ballroom. Below the woman in orange was the name Carol Anthony, alias Catherine Tilley, alias Cassandra Tyler...and the list went on.

"Cassandra Teirney," Montana said. "She was there tonight and none of us saw her."

Lance snorted. "Her hair is a different

color, but it takes a lot more to change the structure of her face."

Kate leaned close to Montana. "Follow her on the video. See who she came in contact with. Maybe she was the one who planted the poison."

Segment by segment, Geek moved through the video. Cassandra made a complete circuit around the room, avoiding the SEAL waiters and managing to remain on the opposite end of the ballroom from Montana and Kate.

"There." Kate pointed. "Is that Abusaid?"

Geek backed up the video several seconds and played it forward slowly.

"There it is again," Kate said. "She stopped to talk with Sayid and shook hands with Abusaid. She didn't shake hands with Sayid."

They watched it again to confirm, and then followed Abusaid as he stood quietly through Kate's speech and the children's choir. Then a waiter carrying hors d'oeuvres stopped beside Sayid and Abusaid. Sayid selected one of the fancy crackers from the tray and popped it into his mouth.

Abusaid declined and the waiter moved on.

The two men chatted and talked with others. Abusaid yawned, covering his mouth with his right hand, and then used the same hand to rub his eyes. He blinked and rubbed them again. He reached out with his left hand to his friend, as if in distress. Sayid hooked his elbow and had him tip his head back. Abusaid refused, seeming unable to open his eyes.

A moment later he clutched his throat and fell to his knees.

The crowd shifted around him, blocking the view.

"He didn't ingest the poison," Montana said. "He rubbed it into his eyes. His body absorbed it faster that way."

"What about Royce?" Lance said. "Back it up. See if he touched Abusaid's hand at any point."

They backed up the video to where Royce entered the ballroom with Tazer. Geek rolled the footage and they followed Royce through the room. He chatted with several people and at one point bent to retrieve something from the floor. When he straightened, Kate gasped. "It's Cassandra, and he's handing her what looks like a glove."

Montana's fists clenched. "The glove with the poison, I'll bet."

KATE COULDN'T BELIEVE this had all happened in front of them and she hadn't seen any of it.

She'd been searching for someone carrying a gun or a detonator.

In the video, Cassandra snatched the glove and turned away as a man stepped up to speak with Royce.

"That's Nigel Carruthers," Mica Brantley said from behind Kate.

She spun to face the woman entering the computer room.

Mica smiled at Kate. "I can't get over how much you look like me." Then she turned back to the monitor. "Nigel was rude tonight. Kate, I don't know how you refrained from slapping his face. I would have, had I been there in person. He had no right to judge my husband."

"Mica." After having the widow in her head all evening, Kate couldn't bring herself to address her as Mrs. Brantley. "Carruthers mentioned something about a project your husband was working on. Did he share any details of his work with you?"

She shook her head. "When he retired from the financial industry, I knew it was a mistake. The man couldn't sit still for long before he was climbing the walls. He said he wanted to do something that made a difference, not just something that made money. He started going out for coffee more often.

Said he was meeting up with friends." She smiled. "I thought he was having an affair."

Kate's heart constricted at the sadness reflected in Mica's eyes.

The widow continued, "When I confronted him with my concerns, he laughed and kissed me, telling me no one could take my place. I was what made everything he did worthwhile. He wanted me to be happy and proud of him. He swore he'd never have an affair with another woman. That he had all the women he wanted in his life with his daughter and me."

That was all any woman wanted to hear. Kate found herself envying what Mica had with her husband.

Mica shrugged. "I believed him. And I still do. He was a terrible liar. When he had secrets he didn't try to lie about them, he made himself scarce to protect us."

"Was he gone a lot?" Montana asked.

"Sometimes he'd leave in the middle of the night and be back in the morning. Other times he'd go out for coffee and not come back until late at night. He said he was working on a project and hoped to tell me all about it someday."

"Do you know who he was working with?" Kate asked.

She shook her head. "No. I was busy organizing sponsors for the gala. I didn't pay much attention after he assured me he wasn't having an affair. Trevor got phone calls. Some of them I answered, and they were from men, not women. Nigel would call as well, to see if Trevor wanted to play golf. Trevor always made time to play a few rounds with Nigel. Then Emily disappeared."

Kate shot a glance toward Geek.

Geek turned to his computer. "Checking phone records."

"I had gone to Paris the week Emily disappeared. I couldn't get a flight home because of weather delays." Tears welled in Mica's eyes. "Trevor and I talked every day, sometimes several times each day. By the time I got home, he was gone, too."

Tears ran down the woman's cheeks.

Kate's chest tightened. The woman had gone through so much, and had been a target herself. It was a miracle she had made it this far.

Brushing aside her tears, Mica straightened. "Trevor also had a cell phone he carried everywhere." She frowned. "I haven't really wanted to go through his things yet, otherwise I might have found it. After the funeral I was in a hurry to get away to find Emily. It was important to me to bring our sweet daughter home. My husband had dropped everything he'd been working on and focused his undivided attention on finding Emily. I'll continue the search until I bring her home."

"How did you find your way to Cancun?" Montana asked.

She brushed fresh tears from her cheeks. "My husband had some clients he'd told me about from his days as a financial analyst. He said they were connected to the Mafia." Mica glanced away. "I got into his records and looked up the names of those clients and paid a visit."

"Were they part of the DC Mafia?" Kate had heard about the crime family. They were reported to be incredibly dangerous. "You went there by yourself?"

Mica shook her head. "Oh, no. I took Rex." Her smile returned. "They were very nice and had nothing but good things to say about how Trevor helped them to invest their money wisely. When they found out I wanted their help to find Emily, they told me about the auction. I knew I couldn't get in as myself, so I had my new friends set me up as a potential client. A *male* client." She smiled across at Duff and Montana. "That's when I met the Navy SEALs. I'm sure I would have botched the whole effort if they hadn't come along when they did."

Kate's head spun. She felt like she'd missed half the conversation. So much more had happened. What had occurred over the past two days, though significant, had been just the tip of the iceberg. No wonder it took an entire whiteboard and timeline to keep track of what was going on.

A phone rang in the room and everyone looked around for the source.

Geek grabbed a receiver from the desktop and answered, "Yeah." He listened for a moment, said, "Will do," and ended the call.

Everyone in the room waited in silence.

He turned to face them. "That was Tazer. Royce is critical, but they think he'll make it. Apparently, he didn't absorb as much of the poison as Abusaid."

As one, they all heaved a sigh.

Montana broke the silence by clapping his hands. "Well, we're not getting paid to look pretty. Let's solve this case and make Royce proud."

Geek returned to his computer to look up phone records.

Kate pulled Mica aside. "Did your husband keep any records at your home?"

Mica shrugged. "Some. We have a safe in the wall. I rarely go in it, except when I need a certain piece of jewelry. He kept our will and the keys to our safe-deposit box at the bank in it."

"Have you cleaned out his files or the safe?" Kate asked.

The widow shook her head. "I really haven't been home since the funeral." She glanced down at her hands. "I haven't had the heart to go back. The house seems so cold and lonely without Trevor."

Kate took the woman's hands in hers. "Would you mind if I go there and have a look around?"

"And me?" Montana laid a hand on Kate's shoulder. "As your bodyguard, I can't let you go alone."

Mica shook her head. "Sure. Go. I'll even give you the combination. You're welcome to go through anything you want. I can't go back. It hurts too much. I keep going over and over in my mind what I could have done differently. I keep thinking that if only I had come home early from Paris, before the storms, Emily might have come to DC to meet me at the airport. She wouldn't have been abducted and Trevor would be alive and here with her. We'd go home as a family."

Kate slipped an arm around the woman's shoulders.

Mica straightened and wiped the tears from her eyes. "Maybe you'll find something the police didn't. A clue as to who did this to Trevor. And, please, look for anything that might point me to Emily. I can't imagine what she's had to endure."

Kate hugged the woman. "I won't make any promises, but we'll try. To the best of our abilities, we'll try." She looked over the top of Mica's head, her gaze capturing Montana's.

The SEAL nodded and, in that one glance, said it all. He was in it to finish it.

Hope swelled in Kate's chest. If anyone could find Emily and bring Trevor's murderer to justice, this team of SEALs and special agents could do it. Kate had to believe it. She didn't care about proving herself and reclaiming her career. Satisfaction would come from helping this woman and avenging the deaths of those who'd fallen.

Kate stood, ready to make it happen.

Chapter Eleven

Montana wasn't keen on going back out into the night after the latest attack, but the only way to solve this case was to take a few risks.

Kate refused to remove the makeup and wig, and claimed that entering the Brantley mansion as Mica would draw less attention or concern from nosy neighbors. However, she did change into dark jeans, a dark sweater and jogging shoes.

"I can't run in a tight dress and high heels, and you won't let me go barefoot," she said as she tied the laces.

Montana chuckled at her logic. He'd removed the torn tuxedo, hoping Fontaine wouldn't be out a lot of money for the damaged rental. He'd had to hit the pavement hard and fast to dodge the bullets aimed his way. Pavement wasn't kind to the fabric that made up a tux.

When they were both ready, he went in search of Geek and Lance, hoping they had some form of transportation they could borrow. He didn't trust a taxi, and the SOS limousine was out of commission.

Lance grinned when Montana approached him with his request. "Do I have some form of transportation you can take to the Brantley estate?" He crooked his finger. "Follow me." He led Montana out to the garage and used a remote control to open an interior overhead door. As the door rose toward the ceiling, Montana's pulse quickened. Inside was a sleek black Ducati motorcycle.

Lance faced Montana, his brows furrowing. "You do know how to ride a motorcycle, don't you?"

Montana nodded. "I learned to ride a motorcycle almost as soon as I learned to ride horses. We used to ride the trails around the ranch on dirt bikes for fun during the summertime."

"Good." Lance crossed to a cabinet, opened it and extracted a black leather jacket and helmet, handing them to Montana. "If those don't fit, there's more where they came from." He opened the door wider, displaying a rack of black leather jackets in all sizes and a row of helmets.

"Good, because Kate's coming with me."

"Has she ever been on the back of a bike?"

"I don't know, but we'll find out soon enough," he said.

Lance grinned. "I'll let her know you're ready and waiting."

Montana selected a jacket and helmet for Kate, guessing at her size. Then he pushed the bike out of the storage area and started the engine. Rather than roaring and rumbling like most of the motorcycles he'd ever ridden, this bike had a muffler system that made it sound like it was a big cat purring with ultimate satisfaction. The vibrations beneath him made him anxious to hit the road. He wished they had time to take the bike out in the country, where he could push it to its limits.

When Kate stepped out of the building, her brows dipped. "Is that our mode of transport?"

Montana, already wearing his helmet with the visor pulled down over his face, nodded. He tossed the jacket into her arms and held the helmet until she was ready for it. "Ever been on a bike?"

"Yes." She slipped her arms into the jacket and propped her fists on her hips. "Have you?"

"Yup." He held out the helmet. "You'll need this, if you're riding with me."

She slipped the helmet over her head and buckled the strap beneath her chin. “And what if I want to drive?”

Montana grinned behind the tinted face shield. Did the woman have any faults? She could take down a grown man, dress like a runway model and command a motorcycle. “I think I’m in love.” The words came out before he could stop them. Once they were spoken, he couldn’t take them back. Instead, he pretended they didn’t mean anything, and scooted back on the Ducati’s seat.

Kate climbed aboard. “My father was an avid cyclist. I think he wanted a boy, but he got me. So he taught me to trail ride by the time I was six and had me competing in motocross competitions by eight.” She revved the engine. “You might want to hold on.”

Any excuse to put his arms around her was good enough for Montana. He cinched his arms around her waist and molded his body to hers.

Lance raised the overhead door.

Even before it was all the way up, Kate drove through, racing out into the street.

Montana had to duck to keep from getting his head knocked off. “Hey! Remember, I’m a little taller than you are.”

"Keep your eyes open, then." She didn't cut him any slack. He didn't really want her to.

If he believed in love at first sight, this would be what it felt like. Kate was amazing. He hoped that after this operation, he'd get to see her again.

KATE HADN'T BEEN on a bike since her father, riding his favorite Harley, was hit by a drunk driver and killed instantly. Her heartbroken mother couldn't stand the sight of her husband's collection of motorcycles. They reminded her too much of her dead husband.

Kate had been in training when her father died. They'd allowed her only a week off to come home for the funeral and then she'd had to report back, or agree to recycle and start all over.

By the time her training was over, her mother had sold all her father's motorcycles for pennies on the dollar and cleared his man-cave garage of all of his trophies. Her mother's grief had taken the form of anger at being left behind. When the anger cooled, she sold the house and moved into a condominium closer to town and went to work for a pediatrician.

Kate loved her mother, but she'd had a special bond with her father that had died when he'd died. Motorcycles would always remind her of him and the joy they'd shared when the wind blew against their faces on the open road.

Kate had committed the route to the Brantley estate to memory from the directions Geek had shown her on the monitor back at SOS headquarters. She leaned into each turn, taking them fast, but controlled.

The SEAL behind her leaned with her, their bodies in tune, like a well-choreographed couple on a dance floor. He knew how to ride. Not all men had experienced the rush of excitement or freedom one could feel on the back of a motorcycle.

All too soon she was gliding to a stop in front of the gated community in which the Brantley estate was located. She punched the code into the box and drove through the gate. A guard stepped out of the booth and waved her to a stop.

She pulled off the helmet, hoping her wig and makeup hadn't rubbed off.

"Oh, it's you, Mrs. Brantley. I didn't know you rode bikes." The guard smiled and backed away. "Good to see you again. It's been a while. Let me know if you need anything. I'm here all night."

"Thank you." Kate drove around the guard

shack and turned left at the first street. The road curved past several massive mansions, each perfectly landscaped with designer bushes and trellises.

Kate pulled into the driveway at the end of the road.

Montana climbed off first and then helped her put the kickstand down.

They walked up to the door together. Montana inserted the key Mica had given Kate and they entered. Kate reset the alarm beside the door and looked around. The foyer was a large open area with marble-tiled flooring and a sweeping, curved staircase leading to the second floor. Kate turned to the right and entered Trevor Brantley's study. Lined in rich wood paneling, the room had bookshelves from the floor to the ten-foot ceilings.

"I'll check out what's in the safe," Montana said. "You take the file cabinet, since you have the key."

"Deal." Kate crossed the room to the built-in file cabinet that blended into the wood paneling. The key unlocked the drawers, allowing her to open them one at a time.

She riffled through file after file, skimming, looking—for what, she didn't know.

Were there any clients he'd had in the past who thought he'd taken advantage of them?

Kate searched for red flags, notes or something that would indicate trouble. Since Trevor had been found in that very study, the police concluded he'd been murdered by someone he knew. There were no signs of struggle. He'd been shot point-blank in the heart and had died instantly.

Kate noticed a dark stain on the Persian carpet in the middle of the floor. She suspected it was Trevor Brantley's dried blood. She wondered if he'd felt any pain or if he'd just ceased to exist. What had been his last thought as the monster who'd claimed his life pressed the gun to his chest?

After going through all four drawers, Kate concluded there were no clues to be found. Not any she could see. She turned to where Montana stood in front of the wall safe Trevor had hidden behind a painting of a racehorse. Her partner was removing documents one at a time, reading through them.

He glanced across at her. "Want to go through them in case I'm missing something important?"

She took the papers and scanned them quickly. One was a will. It had the standard wording, giving Mica everything, with a portion of his life insurance going to his daughter. A trust fund had been set up in Emily's name to pay her a monthly stipend for as long as she lived.

Kate's heart clenched. Emily could already have passed. But until they found her body, Kate refused to believe the young woman was dead.

"Other than the will, a stack of bonds and the key to their safe-deposit box, I don't see anything that raises a flag."

"Then just hand over that key and we can call it a day," a voice said from across the room.

Kate spun to face a woman wielding a pistol with a silencer affixed to the end.

Montana stepped a little ahead of her, placing his body between the woman and Kate. "Cassandra. Or is it Carol? Which did you prefer to go by in prison?"

She snorted. "They called me Bulldog because once I sink my teeth into something, I don't let go."

"I take it you sank your teeth into Brantley and didn't let go until he was dead," Kate said.

Cassandra shrugged. "He was the job. Nothing more. Just like you two are only a means to an end. Brantley refused to give me what I came for."

Kate held up the bank key. "Were you after this?"

Cassandra's eyes narrowed. "If that's the key to the safe-deposit box, yes."

"You know you can't get into it without me," Kate said, glad she hadn't removed her disguise.

"Yeah, well, I know how to get you to co-operate with me." She smiled like she knew a secret.

"And if I don't cooperate?" Kate said.

"Your precious stepdaughter dies." Cassandra lifted a shoulder. "Pretty simple, even for a rich bitch."

Kate's heartbeat rattled against her ribs. "How do I know you're not lying about Emily?"

She lowered her eyelids and gave Kate a sneering smile. "Are you willing to risk her life for whatever's in that box?"

It was Kate's turn to shrug. "I don't believe you have her. I think you're bluffing."

"All I have to do is call and they'd slice her throat." Cassandra's eyes narrowed into slits. "Don't make me mad."

Kate lifted her chin and stared down her nose at the woman. "Give me proof of life and I might give you the key and take you to the bank to let you into the box."

Cassandra's eyes remained narrowed. "How about I just shoot you and take the key?"

"What part of 'you can't get in without me' did you not understand?" Kate asked. "That's how safe-deposit boxes work. You have to have the account holder present to get into it."

Cassandra glared at her. "Don't talk down to me. You're the one on the other end of a gun barrel." She wiped sweat from her forehead.

Kate studied the woman.

Her face was flushed, her eyes bloodshot and red-rimmed. Blood dripped from her left nostril. She raised her arm and wiped the blood away with the back of her sleeve.

"What do you want in the safe-deposit box, Cassandra?" Kate asked.

"*I* couldn't care less about what's in it. The man I work for wants whatever Brantley put in there."

Kate moved forward, holding the key out. "Cassandra—or is it Carol—you don't have to do what that man says. You're sick. You need to get to a doctor."

"I'm fine." She straightened, clutching the

gun in both hands. Her arms trembled, causing the gun to shake. "Just give me the key."

Montana held a slim box in his hand, still standing in the same position he'd been in when Cassandra made her presence known. "You're suffering effects from the poison," he said softly. "Turn yourself in and get some medical attention before it's too late."

"What's it to you? You think I don't know you're one of those muscle-bound jokers who got in my way in Cancun? You and your SEAL friends, living the easy life, vacationing at resorts, sleeping with your favorite flavor of female every day. If I turn myself in, what do I have to look forward to? Going back to jail?" She spat on the floor at Montana's feet. "No way. I make good money working for my boss. I'd rather die than go back to that hellhole."

"You might get your wish," Kate said. "The poison won't stop until you're dead. You saw what it did to Abusaid. If you want to live, you need to get to a hospital right away."

"Abusaid deserved to die. He says he wants peace, but all he really wants is the money to keep flowing, the guns to be delivered and the fighting to continue. As long as his country is at war, he'll continue to make a lot of money."

Kate pressed the woman for answers. "What does Abusaid have to do with Trevor or Emily Brantley?"

"What do any of you have to do with Abusaid, or Senator Houston, or those women I stood to make a crap ton of money on at the auction in Cancun? If you don't see how it all ties together, you deserve to die in ignorance." Cassandra raised the gun with the silencer. By then, her arms shook so badly she could barely keep the barrel parallel to the floor.

Kate bunched her muscles. The woman would have to shoot one or the other of them, but she wouldn't be able to shoot both the way her hands shook.

"You don't owe your boss anything, Cassandra," Kate said, inching across the floor, trying to get close enough to throw herself at the woman. "Go now. Get to a hospital. Choose to live."

"Blah, blah, blah. That's all I hear. Don't you ever shut up?" Blood ran from Cassandra's nose as her gaze narrowed and she shifted her weapon to Kate. "Just die."

Kate dived for the floor, rolled to the right and came up on her haunches.

Something flew through the air, hitting

Cassandra in the face. The gun went off and the next few seconds were a blur of motion.

Montana tackled Cassandra, knocking the gun from her hand. It skittered across the floor, well out of her reach.

The woman lay beneath Montana, her breathing ragged, foam bubbling from the corner of her mouth. "Doesn't matter. He'll get the money any way he has to. You can't stop what he's put in place."

Montana straddled Cassandra's hips, pinning her wrists above her head. "What who put in place?"

Cassandra coughed, blood mixing with the foam dribbling down the side of her face.

"Who are you working for, Cassandra?" Kate asked softly.

Cassandra snorted. "Doesn't matter. You're all going to die." She laughed, the sound turning into a hacking cough.

Montana rose to his feet, kicked the gun farther out of Cassandra's reach and patted down her legs and sides.

Kate walked to the phone on the huge mahogany desk in the middle of the room and dialed 911. "Send an ambulance to this location. We have a woman down. We suspect she's been poisoned."

While Montana stood guard over Cassandra, Kate grabbed a woven throw blanket from a wingback chair and spread it over her. "The poison you used on Abusaid is extremely potent. You might not pull through," she said as she tucked the blanket around Cassandra.

"No one will miss me," she said, her voice cracking, filled with the rattling sound of liquid filling her lungs.

"Why protect the man you work for? He gave you the poison to use, didn't he? Did he tell you it could kill you, as well? Tell me his name, Cassandra," Kate pleaded. "Don't let him get away with killing you."

She stared up at Kate. "He was the only man who ever saw me as anything other than a criminal." Her body shook with the effort. Even after she stopped coughing, she continued to tremble.

Kate nodded. "He must have seen something special in you. Someone he trusted."

"He had to trust me. Anyone else would have turned him in." She smiled and closed her eyes. "Not me. He saved me from spending my life behind bars. He gave me a purpose."

"Who is he?" Kate asked again.

With her eyes still closed, Cassandra whispered, "Your worst nightmare. The judge, jury and executioner." Her words faded and her breathing became shallower.

Kate stared across at Montana, her heart hitting the bottom of her stomach. She couldn't help feeling sorry for the woman, even after she'd tried to kill her. No one deserved to die. Especially such a horrible death, with poison destroying her from the inside.

"What do you think she means by our worst nightmare?" Kate asked.

Montana's lips thinned. "He's been that all along."

Cassandra's mouth moved.

Kate leaned closer to hear the woman's last words.

"You ain't seen nothing yet."

Chapter Twelve

Montana and Kate waited until the ambulance took Cassandra away and the police had processed the crime scene. Nothing they could have done would bring the woman back to life. The poison had taken its toll and put the woman out of her misery and theirs.

Kate had called back to SOS headquarters, reporting what had happened with Cassandra. Becca had taken the call, promising to look more closely at the data they'd compiled on the woman. There had to be some small detail they'd missed that would link her to the man who called the shots.

When the room was clear, Montana held up the key to the safe-deposit box. "We need to touch base with Mica and see what she wants to do about this."

"I'd go to the bank for her," Kate said,

"but I'm sure she'll want to see what's in the box herself."

"Either way, it'll be morning before the bank officials can open the vault. We should call it a day."

As they left the house, Kate seemed distant, almost withdrawn.

Montana wanted to pull her into his arms and hold her, but they'd had a long day and needed to make it back to headquarters and get some sleep. Tomorrow might turn out to be just as difficult. They needed rest to fuel their bodies for the fight.

He slipped his helmet on and waited for Kate to mount the bike.

She buckled her helmet and shook her head. "You drive."

He didn't argue, just took the front seat and waited for her to slide on behind him.

When her arms slid around his middle, he laid his hand over hers and squeezed gently. No words were spoken; just that little bit of skin-to-skin contact was enough for now.

Montana started the engine and drove out of the gated community. As he passed through the streets of DC he was careful to scan the road and side roads in front of him as well as check the rearview mirror. The last thing he wanted to do was lead the assassins back to the SOS building. One bombing in a week was enough.

In the silence of the drive back, he thought through what Cassandra had said. *You ain't seen nothing yet* implied more trouble to come. Possibly on a larger scale than what had already taken place. It didn't bode well for the city of DC.

As soon as he got back to HQ, he'd be sure to check the code dates and coordinates for the next event their tormenter intended to target. Perhaps they'd be better prepared this time and have poison-sniffing dogs there as well as those that sniffed out bombs.

How many ways would the man kill people? And how many mercenaries had he hired to do the job?

After a three-hundred-sixty-degree thorough check, Montana drove up to the overhead door leading into the garage of the SOS alternate site. Not certain how he'd get in, he pulled the helmet off so that the gatekeeper could identify him as one of the good guys. The overhead door opened and Montana drove in.

Once inside, they were met by Becca and Quentin.

"The rest of the gang has bedded down for the night," Quentin said.

"They've already been briefed on the Cassandra situation," Becca added. "Geek's got some information that may or may not be of use."

Montana parked the bike in the storage compartment, set his helmet on a shelf and hung the jacket in the cabinet.

Kate removed and stored her helmet and leather jacket and followed her friend Becca into the building.

Quentin hung back and waited for Montana. "How in the hell did Cassandra get past the gate guard and into the Brantley house?"

"Since we didn't hear her enter, I have to assume she was already there and waiting."

Quentin held the door for Montana. "What gets me is how she knew you two would be there."

"Maybe she didn't. Maybe she was there looking for something, just like us." Montana held up the key to the safe-deposit box. "She wanted this."

Quentin took the key and turned it over in his hands. "You'd think someone would have gone after the safe-deposit box sooner, if it was that big a deal that she'd shoot you for the key."

Montana shrugged. "I certainly don't have all the answers." As they entered the room with the computers, he glanced across at Geek. "What have you got for us?"

Geek pulled up several views on his array of monitors. "I was able to hack into the phone system and look at Brantley's records."

Montana shook his head. "Is there anything you can't get into?"

Geek grinned. "I'm still working on the Chinese military database. It might be easier if I could speak Chinese." He pointed to the monitor on the top right. "These are the phone numbers Brantley called most often. Mrs. Brantley's cell phone, his daughter Emily's cell and these four numbers show up most often. The first two I traced back to burner phones. The kind you throw away when you've used all the minutes. The last two were incoming calls from a local coffee shop."

"Why would a coffee shop be calling Brantley?"

"I asked the same question. I located the shop and looked around it for possible security systems with videos. I struck gold when I found a convenience store nearby that had a clear shot of the front entrance of the coffee shop. I was able to hack into the security system the convenience store uses. God, I love technology."

Geek pointed to another monitor with a blurry image. "On the days Brantley had incoming calls from the coffee shop, I was able to capture images of him arriving fifteen minutes after the call. That's Brantley."

Geek dragged the starting point of the video back twenty minutes. "I wanted to see who'd entered the shop right before the call to Brantley, so I backed it up about thirty minutes and ran it forward." He hit Play and ran the video in slow motion.

Several people entered and exited the coffee shop. Then one man in a jacket, wearing sunglasses and a baseball cap, approached from the opposite direction, his face in full view of the convenience store camera, but the sunglasses hiding his eyes.

"First of all, no one was wearing sunglasses that day, until this guy. That was my first clue he might be the one." Geek zoomed in on the man's face. "He had a scar on his chin that made it look like he had a dimple."

Geek zoomed in even more. "But if you look closely, it's a scar, not an indentation." He moved the cursor and zoomed in on the small, embroidered emblem on the left breast of the man's jacket that read Washington Golf and Country Club. "I could have spent the next two days searching through the registry of the country club looking for someone who could have some connection to Brantley, but Becca walked in about that time."

"What Geek's trying to tell you is that I recognized the jacket, the scar and the man." Becca drew in a deep breath. "That was my father." She bit down on her lip, her eyes suspiciously bright. "Brantley was meeting with my father. I gave my dad that jacket for his birthday last year. He got that scar playing rugby in college."

Quentin slipped an arm around Becca's waist and pulled her close. "We have to assume Brantley's project had something to do with what Marcus Smith and Oscar Melton were working on. Which includes the dates and coordinates, the human trafficking in Cancun and the hits on various, seemingly unrelated people."

Montana stared at the man on the screen. "Which comes back to the question, what did all these people have in common?" He moved to the whiteboard with the names listed, to find a line drawn connecting Brantley to the CIA agents.

"I'm still working on it," Geek said. "I feel like I'm on the verge of connecting all the dots. That is, if we have all the dots on the board."

Becca laid a hand on Geek's shoulder.

"Maybe if you get some sleep, you'll be fresh to start back at it in the morning."

Geek shook his head. "I don't need to sleep. I'm too wound up. I might as well keep going. I want to know who's responsible for all the trouble." His lips thinned. "The boss deserves to know."

Becca turned to Lance, who'd continued to search the internet the entire time Geek was talking. "What about you, Lance?"

"I'm with Geek. I want to know who did this." He and Geek exchanged a glance and nodded. They went back to work, combing through news articles and images.

"Is there anything we can do to help?" Montana asked.

Kate slipped her hand in his. "I can man a computer."

"No, we'd probably just duplicate effort," Geek said. "Besides, you two have been through enough tonight."

Montana led Kate to the office she'd been assigned as her sleeping quarters. "Need help getting out of that wig?"

She shook her head. "I can manage. But I could use some help a little later getting that bed out again."

Montana nodded. "Count on it." He left her

in the hallway and continued to the room he was supposed to be sharing with the guys.

Becca stepped out of one of the offices and blocked his way.

He started around her, but she moved in front of him. "Montana, you got a minute?"

"Sure."

She led him into the office and closed the door behind him. "You and Kate seem to be hitting it off working as partners."

He stiffened. "Yeah. She's smart and knows how to take care of herself."

"There's a reason for that. She's been through a pretty nasty relationship."

He held up his hands. "Whoa. Wait a minute. Are you about to give me the warning about not hurting your friend?"

Becca's cheeks flushed pink. "Yeah. I guess I am." She touched his arm. "I know you're a good guy. I'm just worried about Kate. The mess with Alex nearly destroyed her career and her trust in men."

Montana's lips thinned. He'd like to put his fist through the guy's face. "I'm not Alex."

"I know that. Just don't break her heart. She's been there and done that."

"I've only known Kate for a couple days. When we're done here, I'll be headed back to Mississippi. She's got her work here in DC."

"My point exactly." Becca nodded. "Just keep that in mind. That's all I wanted to say."

Montana turned, reached for the door handle and paused. "How long did it take for you to realize you were in love with Quentin?"

Becca laughed. "Who said I was in love with the self-proclaimed Loverboy?"

Montana faced her, his eyes narrowing.

"Fine. I love the big galoot." Becca sighed. "I knew the day he pulled me out of the alligator-infested swamp in Mississippi. Less than a week after we met. I would have known sooner if I hadn't been so determined *not* to fall for the guy. But our situation is different. We've known each other longer and I wasn't heartbroken by my first love. Kate is fragile."

Montana laughed out loud. "Kate, the woman who could take down a man with one hand tied behind her back and can drive the hell out of a Ducati?"

"I didn't say she was physically fragile. But you don't want to be her rebound guy."

"What do you mean?"

"You know. The guy a girl falls for right after being dumped. Those kinds of relationships don't last."

Montana shook his head. "And you have statistics to back that up?"

Becca shook her head in turn. "No."

"Just so you know, my father was my mother's rebound man after her first husband died from a fatal fall in a rodeo." Montana captured her gaze and held it. "They're still married and more in love than when they first got together. Rebound matches can work. And for the record, Kate's smart, sexy and genuinely good. I'd never break her heart." *But she might break mine.*

Becca gave him a brief smile. "That's all I wanted to hear. Thanks for letting me be a friend to Kate."

Montana hesitated, wanting to be angry with Becca, but understanding why she'd given him *the talk.* "You go right on being a friend. Kate needs them." Montana left the room and continued to the dorm where his stuff was stored. Grabbing a clean shirt and shorts, he headed for the shower and scrubbed away the feeling that he shouldn't go back to Kate's little office with the hide-a-bed. But he'd promised.

KATE HAD MORE trouble removing the wig and makeup than she'd expected. By the time she returned to her room as a natural blonde, it was close to two o'clock in the morning. She entered to find the bed had been pulled out, the sheets smoothed and no Montana.

Disappointment filled her chest. After all they'd been through that day, she'd imagined snuggling with him for the rest of the night. After being shot at, nearly poisoned and run off the road, she wanted…no, she needed the security of his arms around her. Short of marching down the hallway and demanding to know why he hadn't stayed, she didn't have any other choice but to sleep alone.

Kate crawled into the bed and pulled the sheet and blanket up to her chin, feeling more alone than she had since her father died.

Montana had fulfilled his promise to help her with the bed. He was probably supertired and knew if he stayed with her, they'd end up making love again.

Then a horrible thought occurred to her and she shot up to a sitting position. Had he been less than impressed by her lovemaking prowess? Rather than come back again for a second night, was he trying to tell her he wasn't interested?

Kate sank into the mattress. Funny how she hadn't noticed how lumpy it was the night before. She hadn't noticed anything but what Montana was doing to every inch of her body.

God, she missed him. What kind of fool would she be if she fell in love with the SEAL? She had her life as a CIA agent in

Washington, DC. He was stationed in Mississippi, on call and highly deployable to some of the worst hellholes in the world. Any woman would be an idiot to fall in love with a man like that. And he'd be even dumber to fall for a CIA agent with a job such as his.

These thoughts went round and round in her head, keeping her awake for the next two hours. Exhausted beyond insanity, she finally fell into a troubled sleep filled with dreams of friends being poisoned, the people she should have trusted turning against her and the man she feared she was falling in love with walking away without saying goodbye.

By the time she woke the next morning, she felt more exhausted than when she'd gone to sleep. Rather than lie in bed and try to sleep longer, she jumped up, dressed in shorts, a sweatshirt and her running shoes, and went for a jog. Maybe the rush of wind in her face would blow the man from her mind and she could get back to work. *Yeah, and pigs really could fly.*

Chapter Thirteen

Throughout the night, Montana tossed in his bunk, praying he could get even an hour of sleep. By six, he was done trying. He got out of bed and slipped into jogging shorts, a T-shirt and running shoes. He let Lance know he was on his way out and slipped out a side door of the building into an alley.

A few minutes later he was running down the street, headed for the river, hoping for somewhere open and green amid the concrete jungle of the capital.

Once he reached the river, he ran for a couple miles until his body had reached its limit, then he turned around and ran back the way he'd come, pushing himself faster and faster. No matter how hard he worked or how fast he ran, he couldn't get Kate out of his mind. In fact, he could swear he was starting to hallucinate when he saw a woman ahead of him with the same sandy-blond, shoulder-length hair, trim waist and tight calves as Kate.

His pulse quickened and he ran faster. Not until he was less than a block behind her did he realize he was running after a perfect stranger. What would he have done if he'd caught up to her? She might have screamed for the police and accused him of being a stalker.

Montana slowed.

The woman ahead turned at a crosswalk.

Kate.

Montana's heart skipped several beats and then raced, shooting blood and adrenaline through his system like a fire hose at full pressure.

Kate stepped off the curb and jogged across the intersection.

Montana hurried after her, reaching the crosswalk as the red hand blinked a warning to stop. He ignored it and sprinted after her.

Horns honked and a car nearly clipped him as he reached the other side of the street.

Kate glanced over her shoulder at the traffic, spotted him and stumbled. She righted herself and continued to jog, not bothering to slow down and wait for him.

Montana supposed he deserved it for the previous night. She'd more or less invited him to share her bed and he'd been altruistic—sneaked in, pulled out the bed and ran back to his own room before she emerged from the shower. He'd known if he saw her again, he wouldn't be able to walk away.

He told himself he should let her return to headquarters at her own pace, and give her the space she needed. But his body had different ideas.

He ran faster.

Kate sped up, keeping ahead of him, until they were both running all out. By the time they reached the block where the SOS building was located, Montana's lungs and calves burned and he couldn't catch his breath. He slowed, finally giving up. If she didn't want to see him, he shouldn't bust his butt trying to force the issue.

Kate must have come to a similar conclusion at about the same time. She stopped running and bent double, resting her hands on her knees, dragging in deep, gasping breaths.

"Go ahead," she said. "If this is a race, I concede."

Montana joined her and walked the rest of the way to the side entrance of the building. "I'm sorry."

She stiffened beside him. "For what?"

"For not waiting for you to get back from the shower."

Kate shrugged. "Why should you have waited? I asked you to help with the bed and you did. The end."

As they came to a stop in front of the door, Montana gripped her arms and turned her to face him. "I left because I didn't want to take advantage of you."

"Take advantage?" She knocked his hands from her arms. "What kind of man-logic is that?"

"I don't know." He shoved a hand through his sweaty hair. "I'm not a mind reader. I don't know what a woman wants."

"Obviously. When a woman says she wants you to help her with a bed, it's a sign she wants you to stick around to test the springs." Kate turned toward the door, entered the code and let herself in.

Montana followed. "You're still getting over the first man you fell in love with. I'm just your rebound lover."

Kate stopped and turned slowly, shaking her head. "Rebound? Sweetheart, I'm *way* over my first love. In fact, I'm not certain I ever really loved him. Now *you*, on the other hand, are a man and you think just because a woman sleeps with you, she's falling in love with you. Trust me. Just because I slept with you doesn't mean I plan on keeping you around or committing my life to you. I was just looking for a little fun."

Montana's chest tightened. "Is that all? You just want to have fun?"

"Yeah. Then when this is all over, you can go your way and I can go mine. No one gets hurt. Nobody's heart gets broken. Hell, we barely know each other."

"Darlin', you've read me all wrong. I'm not the kind of man who falls in and out of bed so carelessly. *You* might not want to fall in love, but maybe that's what *I* want." He gripped her arms and pulled her against him. "I thought we had a connection. I also thought I was rushing you, so I didn't come to you last night. Not because I didn't want to. Oh, I wanted to. But I didn't want to push you too soon after the hell you'd gone through. Damn it, Kate, I like you. Everything about you, especially kissing you and holding you close. I think you're special, and I want more than just to have fun."

Then he kissed her, his lips crashing down on hers. He pushed his tongue past her teeth and swept the length of hers in a kiss that stole his breath away.

When he was done, he stepped away, dropping his hands to his sides. "That's just who I am. So sue me."

Kate grabbed him around the back of his neck and pressed her finger to his mouth. "Don't you ever shut up?" Before he could answer, she kissed him hard, her tongue searching for and finding his. When she stopped, she backed away, turned and ran.

Montana shook his head. "I don't think I'll ever understand women."

BY THE TIME Kate showered and dressed in jeans and a T-shirt, her pulse had slowed and she could almost make sense of her thoughts again. But no matter how many times she replayed what had happened in the alley, she couldn't believe she'd heard Montana right.

He *wanted* to fall in love?

Most men in his position just wanted to love 'em and leave 'em. Not strings-attached sex. From the beginning, she'd known Montana was different. That's what she loved about him.

Kate passed on breakfast and hurried to the conference room, where she found Geek and Lance hunkered over their keyboards. By the stubble on their chins and the dark circles beneath their eyes, she knew they'd been up all night.

Geek glanced over his shoulder. "Kate. I'm glad you're here. Where's the rest of the gang?"

Becca entered the room. "I'm here. Who else do you want?"

"Everyone. I have something to show you."

Becca left the room and returned with six SEALs, Sam Russell and Natalie. "This is everyone but Fontaine and Tazer. Show us what you've got."

"I knew there had to be a connection to everyone on that board. I just couldn't seem to find it." Geek clicked the keyboard and brought up a view of the Syrian, Abusaid, standing among a group of Caucasians with an American flag on display behind them.

"I did a search on the internet for Abusaid and found this image, taken three years ago at the American embassy in Turkey. Abusaid worked there as a liaison between the Americans and the Syrian government. It was right around that time when there was a car bomb attack at that embassy. Several people were killed in that attack, including this man." Geek pointed to the figure standing beside Abusaid. "That's Patrick Skinner."

Montana shook his head. "Who the hell is Patrick Skinner?"

"Bear with me," Geek said. "I asked the

same thing. But I focused my attention first on the Syrian. I found articles about Abusaid visiting Mexico…" Geek pulled up a media picture of Abusaid standing in front of a huge building in the bright sunshine. "This is him at the Mexican parliament building, and there he is again in Cancun, greeting Mexican officials at one of the posh resort hotels. If you look at the man in the background, surrounded by guys in black shirts, you might recognize him."

Montana's gut clenched. "Carmelo DeVita."

"DeVita, the Mexican drug lord?" Kate asked, leaning close to Montana, her gaze on the monitor.

"He believed in diversifying his portfolio of illegal operations to include drug running, arms sales and human trafficking." Montana's fists clenched. "So Abusaid could have been involved in DeVita's activities."

"Not only *could* he, he *was*. I verified it by going back to DeVita's foreign bank accounts and tracing a link between them and Abusaid's in Turkey. Then I noticed large sums of money moving from Abusaid's account to a Swiss bank account ultimately traceable back to Patrick Skinner."

"Who the hell is Patrick Skinner?" Duff stepped up beside Montana.

"That's where it gets even more interesting." All traces of fatigue seemed to vanish from Geek's face as he warmed to his tale. "Patrick Skinner was the son of multibillionaire Thomas Skinner and his wife, Angela. And get this, Angela brought a son to that marriage and a considerable fortune from her family and her first husband's holdings. You might have heard one of her names. Angela Preston *Carruthers* Skinner."

Montana leaned closer. "Carruthers. Isn't he the man who was all in Kate's face last night at the gala?"

"*Mica's* face. He thought he was talking to Mica," Kate corrected. She walked to the whiteboard and wrote Carruthers's name in the middle of the diagram and drew a line between him and Brantley. Then she wrote Skinner's name and drew lines between Skinner and Carruthers, Skinner and Abusaid, and Abusaid and DeVita. "Carruthers could be our missing link that pulls all of the events together." A chill rippled across her skin and she shot a glance toward Montana. "He could be the one orchestrating this whole operation."

"He could be the one who had been working with assassins to steer the CIA away from what was happening in Cancun."

"Do we have enough evidence to go after him?" Sawyer asked.

Geek shook his head. "Lance and I have been at it all night. All we have are loose connections between Carruthers, Brantley and this Patrick Skinner. We haven't traced any money movement from Carruthers's bank accounts to any of the others."

"All we do know," Lance said, "is that three years ago, he was worth a lot of money. His bank account today is looking pretty bare."

"Do you think he was getting his money to pay the assassins through his connections with DeVita's illegal activities?" Kate asked, feeling excitement building. This could be the break they'd been searching for.

"We don't know at this point."

"We need to find out what's in that safe-deposit box that he wanted so badly," Montana said. He held up the key.

Kate frowned. "I thought you gave that to Quentin last night."

"I did, to keep it safe for the night." Montana glanced toward the door. "Where's Mrs. Brantley?"

"I'm here." Mica entered the room. "What safe-deposit box?"

"We found the key in your home safe last night."

Mica nodded. "Duff was good enough to fill me in on what happened at my house. I'm glad you and Kate made it out all right." She held out her hand.

Montana dropped the key onto her palm.

She studied it. "I hadn't even thought about the safe-deposit box."

Kate's heart twisted. "You had more important things on your mind." She moved to stand in front of the widow. "If you want, I can go to the bank as you and look inside the box."

"No." Mica curled her fingers around the key. "I'll do it. I've relied too much on you already."

"I don't mind at all."

"Let me guess." Mica smiled. "It beats desk duty." The widow pushed back her shoulders and lifted her chin. "I'll go. But I'll need someone to be my Rex."

"I'll go with you," Rex said, stepping into the room behind her. He was still pale and he held his arm close to his side as if he was in a lot of pain from the wound there.

Mica patted his cheek. "Thank you, Rex. You're wonderfully loyal, but I need someone who can run if he needs to. I need you to get well so that you can take up your duties again in the near future."

Rex frowned.

Mica laughed. "Don't worry. I have no plans

to replace you. I like having you around." She returned her attention to Montana. "Since you did such a good job protecting my doppelgänger last night, I'd like you to accompany me to the bank. Do I need to call for my car?"

Montana cast a glance toward Kate.

She grinned and nodded.

Turning back to Mrs. Brantley, Montana asked, "How are you at riding on the back of a motorcycle?"

Chapter Fourteen

It was obvious Mrs. Brantley had never been on the back of a motorcycle. Despite the quick briefing he'd given her, she still didn't understand the concept of leaning into the curve.

They managed to get to the bank unharmed, and Mrs. Brantley met with Mr. Carmichael, the bank manager, to gain access into the vault. She insisted Montana accompany her.

Once inside, they located the box number. The bank manager used her key to unlock it and pull it out of the slot, setting it on a table in the middle of the room.

"Take all the time you need, Mrs. Brantley." The bank manager backed toward the door. "When you're done, use the intercom to let me know you're ready to come out."

"Thank you," she said, her attention already turned toward the contents.

"My husband was a big believer in savings and investments," she said as she lifted out dozens of bond certificates, setting them in a neat stack beside the box. "I guess it's natural for a man who made his living as a financial planner for some of the wealthiest people in this country and abroad." She bit her bottom lip and pulled out a ring box. "Oh my. I thought he'd sold this a long time ago."

"What is it?"

She opened the box. A modest diamond engagement ring nestled in the black velvet. The band was a little dull, but the diamond sparkled, reflecting the overhead lights in a tiny rainbow of colors. "It was my first engagement ring. He'd had to take out a loan to purchase it. When he started making more money, he bought me this one." She held up her hand. On her ring finger was a large square diamond that had to be at least three carats. "I never told him that I preferred the original. He was so proud of himself that he'd done well enough to give me the ring he thought I deserved."

She set the box aside and lifted more papers out. Some were deeds to properties. There were more bonds and stock certificates.

At the bottom of the box was a plain, yellow, legal-sized envelope.

Mica removed the envelope and folded back the metal brads. Two sheets of paper were inside. The first, she handed to Montana. "It appears to be a list of banks and account numbers. By the look of the names, they're Swiss."

Montana studied the paper while Mrs. Brantley read the second document.

Silence stretched between them. When Montana glanced toward the widow, his heart contracted.

Tears streamed down her cheeks and silent sobs shook her body.

He stepped toward her and slipped an arm around her shoulders. "What is it?"

She didn't say, just held out the sheet of paper and pressed a hand to her mouth, the tears continuing to fall as Montana took it from her.

Dearest Mica,

If you're reading this letter, I'm either comatose or have passed. In either case, I'm not around to answer questions. You always left the finances up to me, trusting me to do what was right. You loved and trusted me completely. I hope I've lived up to your trust.

In the event of my demise, I want you to know how very much I love you and wish you to be happy. I don't want you to suffer in any way, and wish for you to go on living a full and happy life. If it means falling in love again, I hope that you will. You are the light of my life and everything I could have dreamed of in a lifelong partner.

Take care of yourself and continue to love Emily like you always have, like the mother she needed.

Give her my love and know that I love you, too. You will be forever in my heart.

Love,

Trevor

P.S. The accounts listed in this packet are where you can find the proceeds from some of my more lucrative investments. I put aside the earnings for a rainy day. There's enough there that you shouldn't have to worry about money for the rest of your life.

Without uttering a word, Montana pulled Mrs. Brantley close.

She buried her face in his shirt and sobbed. For several minutes she poured her heart out in grief. When she had soaked his shirt through, she straightened and looked up at him through red-rimmed eyes. "I'm sorry."

"Don't be. You're allowed to grieve."

"I didn't let myself cry through the viewing or his funeral. I held it together when my heart was breaking into a million pieces. It was the promise I made to myself that I'd find Emily and bring her home that kept me strong." She sniffed and more tears slipped down her cheeks. "And I've failed so miserably."

"It's not over yet," Montana assured her. "We have a lead now. Hopefully, it'll help us find your daughter."

She nodded. "In the meantime, we should take this with us. The stocks and bonds aren't nearly as liquid as Swiss bank accounts. If Cassandra was after something of value, it would be these."

Montana helped Mrs. Brantley replace the paper certificates of stocks, bonds and deeds in the drawer.

Mica slid the ring box into the envelope with the letter and the account numbers, and crossed to the intercom. "We're ready to leave," she said into the speaker.

A moment later the vault door opened and Mr. Carmichael escorted them out.

The ride back to the SOS building was uneventful. Mrs. Brantley held on to Montana, the envelope tucked into her jacket for safekeeping.

Rex met them in the garage, wrapped his

good arm around Mrs. Brantley and ushered her inside, where he supplied her with a cup of hot tea and made her eat some crackers.

After Montana stowed the bike and gear, he returned to the conference room, his heart heavy, his body tense with the need for action.

"How did it go?" Kate turned as he entered.

"It was hard," he said, his jaw tight, his fists clenched. "From the little I know about Trevor Brantley, he was a good man who loved his wife and daughter. He didn't deserve to die."

"Agreed." Kate turned away, but not before Montana saw the mist in her eyes. She stared over Geek's head at the computer monitors. "So what are we going to do about it?"

"We need to check into Carruthers," Montana said.

"Meaning?"

"We need to get inside his house, his business, his anything and find out what he's all about."

"That's breaking and entering," Kate pointed out. "You could go to jail for that."

"Do you think I give a damn about breaking the law? If that man had anything to do with all of the murders, he needs to be stopped before another life is lost."

"So when do we leave?" Duff stepped up beside Montana.

"We need to know where he lives and where his businesses are."

Geek hit a key on his keyboard and a printer spit out a sheet of paper. "Carruthers's home address in Alexandria, his office and warehouse."

Montana's lips quirked upward. "Is there anything you can't do, Geek?"

"I never was much good at tennis," he said, and turned back to his computer.

Duff laid a hand on the computer guru's shoulder. "You and Lance should get some rest. We need you alert and ready to go when we ship out."

Geek nodded. "About to hit the shower, shave and drop for a few Zs. When do I need to be back?"

Montana's eyes narrowed as his resolve strengthened. "Tonight."

KATE SPENT THE day at the computer, monitoring the searches Geek had set up to run automatically. When there was a hit, she checked the data and determined whether it was useful or superfluous. Another application ran in the background, trying every combination of passwords to break into Carruthers's many bank accounts, both personal and corporate.

On the desk beside her, she'd selected an H&K .40 caliber pistol as weapon of choice for the reconnaissance that evening. She'd assembled, disassembled and reassembled it four times. Then she'd cleaned, oiled and fitted it into a shoulder holster she'd strap on when they were ready to move out.

Becca leaned over her shoulder and set a steaming mug of coffee in front of her.

The aroma filled her senses and she inhaled deeply. "You read my mind."

"Have you talked with Mica since she returned from the bank?" Becca asked.

Kate shook her head. "She looks so sad, I'm afraid I'll make her cry again if I ask her how she's doing."

Becca's lips tightened. "I take it you read the letter."

Kate nodded. Every time she thought about it, her throat constricted and her eyes stung. "We need to find Emily."

"Mica's spent a fortune chasing leads. What makes you think we'll have any more luck?" Becca asked.

"She didn't look right here at home." Kate lifted the pistol and weighed it in her palm. She'd had one like it in her apartment. Her father had given it to her for her nineteenth birthday and spent the day at the range with her, teaching her how to handle it properly. "That poor girl has been gone for weeks. Can you imagine what she's had to endure?"

Becca shook her head. "I don't want to."

"I don't, either." Anger burned inside Kate. "She needs to be home with her mother."

"I'm afraid to leave Mica here tonight."

Kate looked up into her friend's face and read the concern etched into the lines on her forehead. "Why?"

"I'm afraid she might take matters into her own hands and go after Carruthers."

"We don't know for certain Carruthers is our man," Kate argued.

"Exactly." Becca's lips twisted. "And going outside these doors without Rex or another bodyguard is too dangerous."

"What do you propose?"

"One of us needs to stay with her at all times."

"What about Rex?" Kate asked.

"Mica insisted he take a painkiller. I think he's down for the night."

"What about Geek or Lance?" Kate didn't want to stay behind and look after Mica when the others would be out in the field, possibly cornering the bastard who'd put them all through hell.

"Geek will be manning operations from here. Lance and I are operating the communications van." Becca smiled. "I'm driving."

Kate sighed. "Which leaves me." She glanced at the gun, knowing it wouldn't be used that night. "Why me, and not one of the guys?"

"Fair question. I think she would appreciate a female shoulder to lean on right now."

"Tazer?"

Becca shook her head. "She refuses to leave Royce in case the poison attack on him wasn't just an accident of picking up the glove." Becca laid a hand on Kate's shoulder. "You've been Mica. You've had her inside your head. You practically know what she's thinking."

Much as Kate hated to admit it, she was the logical choice to stay with Mica. If the woman was contemplating making an attempt to see Nigel Carruthers, someone had to be there to stop her.

"So, will you stay?" Becca asked.

"We'll see." Though her answer was noncommittal, she knew what she had to do.

The six SEALs and SOS agent Sam Russell prepared a battle plan. Geek and Lance would provide the tech support they'd need for communications and to bypass security.

Geek had already hacked into Carruthers's security service and was prepared to shut it down for the time needed for the SEALs to get in and out of the man's house.

The men dressed all in black and wore soft-soled dark shoes and ski masks. They carried pistols and stun guns, prepared to use whichever the situation warranted.

"Just remember," Sam reminded them, "this isn't a foreign country, and we aren't under wartime rules of engagement. If we're caught, we face the possibility of going to jail for breaking and entering. Anyone who wants to opt out, do so now. Once we go in, we're committed."

None of the men left the room.

Becca must have let them know that Kate would be staying behind to assist Geek and protect Mica, because they didn't include her in the planning.

She wanted to be a part of the team that found the evidence that would nail the guy who'd killed so many. She wanted to be there when they took him down.

"And, men," Sam continued, "if you locate Emily, bring her home."

The team loaded into the communication

van. Becca would drive while Lance manned the electronics. Once they were within half a mile of their target, Sam and the SEALs would disembark and continue on foot.

Montana was the last to climb into the van.

Kate caught his arm before he stepped in. “Hey.”

He paused with one foot in and the other on the ground. “Hey, yourself.”

“When you get back, we should talk.” Kate wanted to say so much more, but the guys were waiting. “Okay?”

Montana nodded. “You bet.”

She started to back away, but Montana grabbed her arm and pulled her close, capturing her mouth with his. His kiss was brief, but warm, and promised more when he got back.

Quentin, Sawyer, Duff, Hunter and Rip whistled and teased him as he climbed in and the door slid shut.

Kate didn’t care what anyone thought but Montana. She hadn’t known him long, but one thing was sure, she could very easily fall in love with the man, and might already be halfway there. The thought of him going to a place that could be teeming with assassins made her wish she had gone along. She could have had his back. Mica had taken care of herself thus far, and could make do for one more night.

Then again, Mica hadn't read the letter before today, nor had she allowed herself to grieve for her dead husband until now. Grief made people do things they wouldn't normally do, like sell every last motorcycle in her husband's treasured collection.

Kate returned to the conference room, where Geek was talking into his mic, performing a comm check with each member of the team. When Montana checked in, Kate's pulse quickened.

She told herself he'd be back soon enough. They'd talk. They might even make love, if she convinced him she really wanted him to stay for the night, and that he wouldn't break her heart.

Yeah, they had a few things to discuss. Number one on the list was where their relationship was going.

Kate wandered out into the corridor in search of Mica. Rex was as Becca suspected, passed out in the men's dorm, doped up on pain medication.

She found Mica in the little kitchen, sitting at a table, nursing a cup of tea and rereading the letter her husband had left.

Kate poured a cup of coffee, carried it over to the table and sat across from her.

Mica sniffed. "He really did love me."

"Yes. He did," Kate agreed. "I hope someday to find a man who loves me as much as your husband loved you."

Mica glanced up with bloodshot, red-rimmed eyes. "Until now, I hadn't stopped long enough to consider living life without Trevor. Today is the first day it really hit me."

Kate didn't know what to say to her. How did you console someone who was deeply and utterly heartbroken? She reached across the table and placed her hand over Mrs. Brantley's.

"I miss him," she whispered.

"My dad and I were really close," Kate said. "When he passed away, I couldn't imagine life without him in it. He was my rock. I always knew he would be there to catch me if I fell. When he died, it took a long time for me to regain my balance, but I did."

Mica looked up. "How did you get over the loss?"

Kate smiled and shook her head. "I didn't. He's still that big part of my life that I will never forget. He's with me every day." She patted her chest. "I carry him in my heart. The memories we shared, good and bad, are all there. I take them out and examine them occasionally when I run across something that reminds me of him."

They sat for a long while in silence.

When Mica drank the last drop of her tea, she stared into the cup as if wondering where it had all gone. Then she sighed. "I think I'll go lie down for a while. You will come get me if you hear anything, won't you?"

"You bet," Kate said. She took both their cups to the sink and rinsed them, then walked Mica to her room. "If you need me for anything, even an ear to bend, I'm here for you."

Mica smiled. "Thank you. You've been more than kind to a woman you didn't even know."

"I just wish I could do more."

Mica hugged her, tears filling her eyes. She hurried into her room and closed the door.

Kate returned to the conference room, her heart hurting for the woman who'd lost her entire family.

Geek was staring at a monitor with several green dots, each with a name assigned. "They're on the Carruthers estate grounds, moving up to the main house."

Kate leaned close, her pulse rushing through her veins. What she wouldn't give to be with them. She could almost smell the gardens and taste the night air.

Geek pressed some keys. "Security system has been disabled at the house with a false signal feed to the security provider." Geek sat back. "Now all they have to do is get inside without being detected, find some evidence and get back out without being shot." He shook his head. "God be with them."

Kate sat on the edge of her chair, her breath caught in her throat. The silence stretched between them as they watched the green dots move into the mansion.

A sound behind her made Kate jump. She turned to find Mica standing in the doorway, her face pale, her eyes wide.

Kate leaped from her chair and ran to the woman. "What's wrong?"

The widow held up her cell phone. "He wants to make a trade. Emily for the Swiss accounts access codes."

Chapter Fifteen

Montana moved through the house, treading lightly, careful not to bump into anything or make a sound. From all Geek and Lance could find online, Carruthers didn't own a dog. There were no payments made to a veterinarian and nothing they could find that indicated he spent money on dog food bills. That didn't mean he didn't have one. So far, they hadn't been attacked or had an animal barking to raise the alarm.

Once inside, the team split up. Duff and Sawyer went up the sweeping staircase. Rip and Hunter had the main floor, while Montana headed to the basement. Quentin and Sam Russell had bypassed the house to check the outbuildings and the additional three-car, detached garage. Their goal was to be in and out in less than ten minutes. With an office building and warehouse yet to visit that night, they had a lot of ground to cover.

Montana found the doorway to the basement tucked beneath the staircase leading up to the second floor. The door had a keyed lock on the outside, which made the hairs on the back of Montana's neck stand on end. He pulled out his Swiss Army knife, unfolded the thin, hardened, stainless steel file and inserted it into the keyhole.

After several twists and feeling his way around, he found the sweet spot and disengaged the lock. Pushing his night-vision goggles down over his eyes, he descended the steps into the basement.

Halfway down, one of the boards creaked. Montana paused and listened for any sign that the basement was occupied. Nothing moved and complete silence reigned.

Continuing to the bottom, he paused and looked around. His goggles picked up a heat source, which turned out to be the water heater. Another source was the pilot light for the central heating unit. Other than that, the room was cold.

Montana pushed the goggles up and clicked on his small flashlight. The floor space equaled the size of the first floor, with eight-foot ceilings and a massive system of wine racks lined up to the back wall. Most of the racks were empty and laced with cobwebs. The two windows the basement sported had long since been bricked over.

Other than stacks of old furniture and boxes, Montana didn't see much that interested him. Still, he checked behind the furniture and boxes, careful to search for hidden doors. The boxes and crates contained vintage clothing and knickknacks from what appeared to be the sixties or seventies. Thankfully, he didn't find any skeletons or bodies among the refuse.

Montana checked the wine racks one by one, finding nothing but dust and spiderwebs. Strangely, the main path leading past them had many footprints, displacing the layers of dust.

Adrenaline spiked in his blood as Montana eased forward, his weapon drawn. He clicked off the flashlight, lowered his night-vision goggles and passed the last rack, to find another door at the very back of the room, tucked behind it. Only this door was short, only five feet tall at the most, and it, too, had a lock on the outside and several shiny new dead bolts, all engaged.

Whatever Carruthers stored in here, he didn't want getting out.

Montana pressed his ear to the solid wood door, but couldn't detect any sound inside. Raising his night-vision goggles again, he clicked on his flashlight and checked all around the seams for anything that might trigger an explosion.

When he was fairly certain it hadn't been booby-trapped, he unlocked the dead bolts, one at a time, careful not to make noise. Again he applied his file to the door lock. This one took a little more time, but he finally found the right spot and disengaged the lock.

Stepping out of the entryway, he pulled open the door and aimed his weapon at the interior. His breath caught and held as he waited for movement, but none came.

With one hand holding his gun and the other a flashlight, he shone light into the tiny space. The majority of the room was filled with a cot bolted to the concrete floor. On it was a thin mattress and a single blanket. In one corner was a gallon tin bucket, in the other a collection of empty water bottles and food wrappers. Hanging on hooks screwed into the wall was a pale pink blouse, covered in dirt and grime. A Washington Redskins hooded sweatshirt hung beside it.

Montana swore and then spoke softly into

his radio headset. “I think I found where the bastard has been keeping Emily.”

Within seconds, three of the six other men converged on the basement.

Montana snapped pictures of the blouse and sweatshirt. He’d have Mica verify whether or not they belonged to Emily.

Looking closer, they discovered several long, blond hairs on the blanket. Montana was confident if they ran a DNA test on those hairs, they’d prove the person held captive in this room had been Emily Brantley.

They were all very careful not to touch the evidence. Montana and the rest of the SEAL team had worn gloves to avoid leaving any fingerprints or destroying other fingerprints throughout the house.

Carruthers wasn’t home and, based on how fresh some of the food wrappers were, Emily hadn’t been gone from her cell for long.

As they emerged from the house into the open, the team converged and moved toward the fence they’d scaled on their way in.

“We need the police on this house ASAP and an all-points bulletin out on Carruthers,” Montana said into his mic. “Lance, any idea where Carruthers could be right now?”

“He might have moved her to one of his other buildings. Since the office building is in downtown DC, my bet would be he took her to the warehouse."

"Uh, gang, we have a problem," Geek said into Montana's ear.

"What?" Montana asked, his stomach clenching.

"Mica and Kate are on their way to meet with Carruthers."

"Say again?" Montana demanded. "I thought Kate was going to keep Mica there."

"Yeah, well, as of five minutes ago, they left, asking me to give them a head start. Carruthers called Mica and offered a trade. Emily for the Swiss bank account codes. She's to arrive alone. They took the bike."

Montana swore, his heart pounding against his ribs as he imagined Kate racing through the night toward what Montana was certain would be a trap.

The SEAL team reached the eight-foot-tall concrete block fence and assisted each other over the top, one by one. The van waited on the other side of the street.

Once they were all inside, Montana leaned over Lance's shoulder, stared at his computer monitor and spoke into his radio headset. "Tell me you sent them with trackers."

Geek responded, "Absolutely. Bringing them up now."

Lance's screen blinked and two green dots appeared amid an outline of the Washington city streets.

"They're headed toward the river," Lance said.

"On it," Becca called out from the driver's seat.

They raced toward the capital, headed north from Carruthers's estate in Alexandria.

"Not good," Lance said. "Look, they're following the river, but heading due south toward the convergence of the Potomac and the Anacostia Rivers."

"Carruthers's warehouse isn't in that direction," Geek said.

"What else *is* there?" Montana asked.

"I believe Carruthers owns a boat or a yacht," Geek replied. "They could be headed for the James Creek Marina. Want me to call in the police?"

"They might get there before we can," Duff said.

"And you said she's supposed to show up alone." Montana didn't like it. "Calling in the police could put them in even more danger." He looked down at the map on Lance's screen. "Where's the closest marina to us?"

Lance brought up another screen and

searched for marinas. "There. Two miles ahead on the right."

"Head for it. We can get to the James Creek Marina quicker by water," Montana said. "And if Carruthers takes them aboard his boat, we can pursue in one of our own."

"And where do you propose we get one at this hour?" Duff asked.

Montana's jaw hardened, but he didn't respond.

Duff sighed. "That's what I was afraid of. We can add grand theft watercraft to breaking and entering on our rap sheet." He clapped his hands together. "What are we waiting for?"

Becca drove like a wild woman, coming to a screeching halt at the marina.

Montana pointed to his teammates. "Duff, Sawyer and Quentin, you're with me. The rest of you try to make it to the marina by road and head them off if Carruthers makes a run for it by land." Montana was first out the van door.

He'd gone boating in Montana in an old fishing boat his grandfather kept together with spit and glue. He'd had to manually start the engine on more than one occasion, which was pretty much what he'd had to do for most of the old farm machinery around the ranch. He had skills that weren't part of his résumé, and he planned to use them to rescue Kate, Mica and Emily.

Montana sprinted toward the last row of boats, hoping to get away before an alarm was sounded. A locked chain-link gate blocked his entrance to the boat slips.

"Want me to go back to the marina and see if I can find bolt cutters or a pry bar?" Duff asked.

Montana shook his head. The van had left as soon as the team of four had disembarked. They'd spend more time looking for something to break through the combination lock on the gate than going around. He shrugged out of his gear, shirt and shoes, and handed everything to Duff, including his radio headset. "I'll be right back."

"Uh-huh," Duff said. "And we'll be waiting here as your accessories to the crime."

Montana dived into the murky water of the Potomac River and swam around to the boat slips, where he pulled himself up onto the dock. He looked for the fastest craft that could carry the four of them and climbed down onto the bow. Before he attempted starting the engine without a key, he checked the glove box and beneath the seats. Luck shone down on him when he found the keys to the boat in the storage well beneath a bench seat. In seconds, he had the boat untied, engine running and pulled around to the ramp where the others of his team waited.

A quiet *hoo-yah* sounded off and they all piled in.

Duff took over driving the boat as Montana dried his face with his shirt and reestablished communications with headquarters and the comm van.

"Where are they now?" he asked, shivering in the cool night air.

"They stopped at the marina," Geek replied.

"The van's ETA is about fifteen minutes the way Becca drives," Montana reported. "Four of us are going by water. ETA less than five minutes."

"Good," Geek said. "I'll let you know when they're moving again."

Montana fought the urge to take the helm from Duff. But Duff was the best boat driver on SBT-22. Instead, Montana moved to the front of the ski boat and searched the water ahead for boats coming or going. Since they were in a stolen boat, Montana hadn't wanted to turn on the running lights and alert harbor police to their presence. They didn't have time to be stopped, and he had no desire to play hide-and-seek with the authorities any sooner than he had to.

"You should see the light on Hains Point coming up, dead ahead," Geek said into Montana's headset.

The moon shone down on the water, giving Montana a clear view of the convergence of the two rivers. He could see the spit of land separating the Potomac from the Anacostia. "I see it."

"Steer right of the point and you'll see the next one, Greenleaf Point," Geek instructed. "James Creek Marina is just past it."

"Got it." Montana counted the seconds, praying they got there in time. With Carruthers's ruthless disregard for life, he might decide to shoot all three of them, take the codes and leave the country.

Montana couldn't let that happen. He liked Mica. The woman was strong, dedicated to her family and genuinely good. And Kate…

He was already halfway in love with her. He needed more time to convince her she could love him, too. Yeah, his career in the Navy would make it hard to date, but he really wanted to see Kate. He'd make the sacrifices necessary, if given the chance.

KATE STOPPED SHORT of the James Creek Marina, the last place the man who'd called Mica had given them on their scavenger hunt through the city. Since Mica was supposed to arrive by herself, she'd have to go in on foot. Kate would ditch the bike and follow at a little bit of a distance, swing around and try to come at the kidnapper from the side.

She'd bet the man was Carruthers. After listening to the instructions with the phone on speaker, she would recognize that voice as Carruthers's from his rude remarks at the gala. The man was insane, which didn't bode well for Emily.

Mica couldn't be dissuaded from delivering the codes herself. She didn't want Carruthers to have any excuse to execute her stepdaughter. Kate suspected Carruthers had no intention of letting either one of them leave alive. He'd killed, or paid to have killed, too many people to leave any loose ends running around with his name on their lips.

Dressed in dark jeans and a dark shirt, with her hair stuffed up into a black hat and her skin covered in black camouflage paint, Kate hugged the bushes and buildings, moving swiftly and quietly through the shadows. She carried the .40 caliber H&K pistol, and a sniper scope and rifle with a removable butt she'd reassembled once she'd dismounted the bike.

Mica walked down the road toward the

marina, carrying the page of account access codes tucked into her back pocket. Though shaken by the call, she'd held up pretty well, with the chance of getting Emily back giving her the hope and determination to face the killer.

Mica had promised to move slowly, giving Kate time to position herself to take a shot if the need arose. The caller had instructed her to walk out on the dock and wait for additional instructions.

Geek had equipped Kate with a single-lens, night-vision monocular. As she moved toward the wide-open space on the approach to the marina, she lifted the monocular to her eye and scanned the area for the telltale green heat signature of a warm body.

Immediately, she noted a figure leaning against the far side of the marina and another on the closest corner.

"Damn," she muttered beneath her breath. It would take some doing to reach either one without alerting them to the fact Mica that was not alone. All Kate could hope for was that their attention would be on Mica.

Swinging wide, Kate came at the marina on the far side, hopefully sneaking up behind the man on the back corner.

Clouds skittered across the half-moon, giving Kate additional concealment as she raced across an open area and ducked behind a storage shed. Rather than confront the sentry guarding that end of the marina, she slipped behind the building and peeked around the corner toward the dock.

A large man stood on the wooden planks, his arm wrapped around the neck of a young woman.

Emily.

Kate's pulse quickened.

"Don't do it, Mom," the girl called out. "He's lying about letting me go."

"Shut up," the man said, and clamped a hand over her mouth.

Emily bit his palm.

The man hit her in the side of the head and she went limp.

"Emily!" Mica said, increasing her pace until she was running toward the man who held her stepdaughter.

When she was within ten yards of the two, the man said, "Stop."

Mica slowed to a stop, breathing hard. "Don't hurt her. I have the codes. Let her go, and I'll give you them."

"How do I know you have the codes?" the man asked.

Mica dug in her back pocket and pulled out

the sheet of paper, then held it over the side of the wooden dock. "Let her go, or they go in the water."

"If you do that I have no reason to let you or the girl live."

"Nigel," Mica said, her voice clear and calm. "She's done nothing to hurt you."

"My brother did nothing to hurt you and your family, but your husband was determined to smear his name, even after he was dead."

"I don't know what you're talking about. What Trevor did has nothing to do with Emily. She's innocent."

"Nobody is innocent. Nobody comes out of this world alive. We all die."

"Nigel..." Mica spoke in a soft, insistent voice. "It's over. You can't continue to kill people."

"Why not? Abusaid's people killed my brother. Our government didn't protect him. Patrick was my only family member. Everyone who had a hand in what happened needs to pay for what they did, or what they refused to do. And they're going to pay with their lives and those of their families. They should have cared."

"Please, let Emily go," Mica begged.

He tightened his grip on Emily and his voice grew harder. “Give me the codes.”

Mica stepped closer. “Release Emily.”

“Not until I have the money,” Carruthers said.

Kate lifted the rifle to her shoulder and set her sight on Carruthers. Emily’s head and body were in the way of a clear shot at the man.

“That will take time,” Mica said. “You’ll need access to a computer.”

“Then you’ll have to come with me.” He spun and dragged Emily toward the long, sleek yacht behind him. A man emerged from the shadows, grabbed her and tossed her on board.

Emily scrambled to her feet and rushed toward the side of the vessel. As she bent to spring out into the water, a man grabbed her from behind. She screamed.

The man clamped a hand over her mouth and dragged her inside.

“Emily!” Mica rushed forward.

Carruthers grabbed her arm and twisted it up between her shoulder blades. “Come on, Mica, we’re going for a little ride.” He yanked the page of codes from her hand and shoved her toward the yacht.

Kate aimed at the back of Carruthers’s

head as he shoved Mica toward his waiting henchman.

"I wouldn't do that if I were you," said a coarse voice behind her. She turned to look down the long barrel of an AR-15 rifle, with a tall, mean-looking man at the other end, ready to shoot. "Drop the weapon and get up."

Kate laid the rifle on the ground, but as she rose, she brought it up with her and slammed it into the man's groin.

He cursed and swung a meaty fist, hitting her in the side of the head. She staggered backward and into the arms of another one of Carruthers's goons.

He clamped his arms around her, pinning her arms to her sides, and lifted her off her feet. Kate kicked and fought, but the guy had her in a pinch she couldn't wiggle her way out of. Between the two men, they carried her on board the yacht and the boat pulled away from the dock.

Carruthers waved his hand toward the interior of the yacht. "Throw her in the room with the other women, bring my laptop and get us the hell out of here."

The men carried Kate through a doorway and down a stairwell to the cabin area below. One of them opened a door, and she was tossed into a small room.

Mica held a dirty, disheveled Emily in her arms. Tears streamed down both their faces.

As soon as she hit the floor, Kate scrambled to her feet and ran back to the door. But it shut in her face, and she heard the sound of a lock clicking in place.

She didn't waste time trying to twist the knob. She had to find something with which to pick the lock or pry the door open. The cabin consisted of two bunks, one over the other, and a built-in dresser. Kate ran for the dresser and yanked out a drawer.

"What are you going to do?" Mica asked.

"Get us out of here." Kate slammed the drawer against the bunk, breaking it into pieces.

Mica let go of Emily and straightened. "How can we help?"

Chapter Sixteen

As the ski boat approached Greenleaf Point, a yacht passed them, fifty feet away on their starboard bow.

"Kate and Mica are on the move again." Geek's excited voice filled Montana's headset. "They just passed you on the river, headed the opposite direction."

Duff waited for the yacht to clear them, staying close to the bank. The clouds chose that moment to provide concealment from the other vessel. Once the big yacht passed, Duff swung wide and fell in behind it.

"Montana and Quentin, get ready to board," Duff called out. "Sawyer, cover."

The men took their places. Montana and Quentin hunkered low in the front of the boat until they were right behind the yacht, riding in the bigger boat's wake. The roar of the yacht's engine covered their motor noise.

With luck, the occupants wouldn't ever expect someone to board them while they were moving.

Duff eased up in the churning wake. When they were close, he shoved the throttle forward a hair more, practically riding up on the back deck.

Montana leaped from the bow and landed on the yacht's back platform. Quentin landed beside him and Duff slid away to the rear and swung wide, coming up on the starboard side.

Sawyer yelled, loudly enough for the yacht occupants to hear, "Hey, jerkface! Wanna race?"

While the attention was on Sawyer, Montana climbed onto the deck. A man carrying a gun looked over the side at the ski boat keeping pace with the yacht in the dark.

Montana sneaked up behind the man and hit him hard on the back of the head with the butt of his .45 caliber pistol. The man went down.

Quentin was there to zip-tie his wrists and ankles and jam a cloth into his mouth. Together they lifted him up and stowed him in a rubber dingy, covering him with several life vests.

Montana and Quentin eased around the port side, while Duff, in the ski boat, zigzagged close to the yacht's starboard side, with Sawyer yelling like a drunk man.

Montana found an open, sliding glass door leading into the luxury yacht. He eased up to it and peered in.

Across the lounge, a man wearing a tailored suit and carrying a gun stood beside a thin man in thick glasses hunched over a computer, cursing. Montana recognized the suited man as Nigel Carruthers.

The computer guy cursed again. "Damn it! These codes aren't getting me in."

"You better hope they do," said Carruthers. "If you don't get the money transferred by midnight, we don't get the activation key."

"I'm working on it. Give me time."

"You said you could make it happen if you had the accounts and passwords. What's the holdup?" Carruthers demanded.

"In addition to the codes and passwords, there are prompt questions I don't have the answers to."

Carruthers waved toward the door where Montana was standing. Two men stepped forward. Each was dressed like a member of an elite military force, in matching black outfits, and they carried military-grade AR-15 rifles.

"Get Mrs. Brantley," Carruthers ordered.

Both men executed an about-face and walked out of Montana's view.

Once Carruthers turned back to the man at the computer, Montana dared to stick his head through the door. He saw the hired guns descending a staircase into the lower level of the big yacht.

A voice sounded over an intercom. "Sir, we might have a problem out here."

Montana held his breath, praying Quentin or the disabled guard hadn't yet been discovered.

Carruthers hit a switch on an end table. "Can't you handle it? We've got bigger fish to fry in here."

"We have company off the starboard bow. A small boat, running without lights."

"Authorities?" Carruthers asked.

"No. It appears to be a couple of drunk guys on a joyride."

"Run them over, shoot them. I don't care. Just get rid of them."

Montana almost laughed at the description of Sawyer and Duff. Their diversion had bought the two SEALs on board precious time to locate their opponents and neutralize them.

Montana was certain he could handle those

inside the yacht. He only hoped Quentin didn't run into heavy resistance on the outside.

Since the men went down under to retrieve Mrs. Brantley, it stood to reason the other two ladies were below, as well.

Gunfire sounded from below.

"Damn it! We don't need this now. They're going to bring every member of the port authority out to investigate." Carruthers kicked the back of the computer guy's chair. "We're running out of time." He glanced toward the stairwell. "What the hell is going on down there?" Louder, he yelled, "You better not shoot Mica Brantley! I need her to break this code!"

KATE HAD STRIPPED a metal slide off the broken drawer and rammed it into the door casing. Unfortunately, the builder had spared no expense and built the framing strong enough to withstand a pirate attack. After bending two slides, she searched for something small enough to slip into the lock. The only thing she could think of was the underwire on her bra.

She stripped off the bra and ripped the wire out. Kate had the wire in the lock when a key pushed in from the other side.

"Someone's coming in," Mica whispered.

Kate spun away from the door, grabbed one of the long splinters from the broken drawer and hid it behind her back.

Mica released her grip on Emily, and the two women grabbed other strips of wood, tucking them behind their backs, as well.

The door slammed open.

A big guy dressed in all black pointed at Mica with a pistol. "You. Upstairs."

Mica shot a glance at Kate, who was standing closer to the door and the man with the gun.

Kate gave a slight nod. When Mica passed her, she edged forward.

The man half turned to leave, giving Kate her opportunity.

She leaped forward and stabbed her splinter into the man's hand holding the gun.

He cursed, flung the weapon to the floor and clutched his hand to his chest.

"Mica, Emily, drop!" Kate yelled, as she dived for the gun.

Mica and Emily dropped to the floor as another man burst into view with his pistol.

Mica stabbed the guy in the calf.

Grabbing the gun off the floor, Kate turned onto her back and fired at the man, hitting him in the chest.

He staggered backward but didn't go down,

indicating he was wearing protective body armor. Kate fired again, hitting the guy in the neck.

The man whose hand she'd stabbed reached down and grabbed a hank of Mica's long black hair and dragged her to her knees.

Kate didn't hesitate; she pulled the trigger. The bullet hit Mica's assailant square in the face. He fell backward and lay still.

Mica jumped up and ran for Emily, pulling the younger woman into her arms.

Kate rolled to her feet and ran for the door. Their only hope was for her to fight her way out of this. After she'd killed Carruthers's thugs, Kate knew he wouldn't let her live.

MONTANA STARTED ACROSS the lounge toward Carruthers when the man at the computer shouted, "I'm in!"

"Quick! Transfer the money." Carruthers slammed his palm against the back of the man's chair. "Hurry, damn you!"

"Doing it now." The computer guy pressed a button and stared at the screen. "Transferred!" He pounded the keys again and sat back. "We have the firing key."

"Enter it! Do it!" Carruthers screamed.

Montana stepped up behind the man and

pressed his gun to Carruthers's head. "Stop whatever it is you're doing or I'll shoot you."

The computer guy jerked around in his seat so fast he fell backward.

Carruthers swung, slamming his hand into Montana's arm, but didn't succeed in dislodging the gun.

Montana brought his fist upward in a powerful uppercut, caught the man in the chin and knocked him flat on his back. Then he straddled him and pressed his .45 to his captive's cheek. "It's over, Carruthers. You're done terrorizing others."

Lying on his back, Carruthers smirked. "You're right, I'm done. In exactly two minutes, all of DC, its crooked politicians, lobbyists and political action committees will be blown off the map."

"What are you talking about?" a female voice said from behind them.

Out of the corner of his eye, Montana could see Mica, Emily and Kate. His chest swelled, filling with joy. Kate held a gun on Carruthers. Mica and Emily held splinters of wood like battle swords.

Carruthers looked past Montana to Mica, and his smile became a sneer. "You thought you could save your stepdaughter, but what you didn't know is that you would be dying with her. The irony is I used *your* money to purchase the key to activate a dirty bomb located so close to the capital, nobody will get out alive." He laughed. "You have less than two minutes. Say your goodbyes."

Kate stepped forward. "What have you done?"

The man on his back shook his head. "What someone should have done a long time ago. I'm taking a bomb straight to the nation's capital and it's too late to stop it."

Montana's heart stopped for a second and then raced ahead. "You have a bomb on this boat?"

Carruthers chuckled. "Even if you find it, you can't disarm it."

Montana leaped to his feet. "Kate, take him. We have a bomb to find."

About that time, the yacht came to a stop. Quentin appeared in the doorway. "Guards have been neutralized and the captain is unconscious." His eyes narrowed. "What's going on?"

"Carruthers has a dirty bomb on board. We have a minute to find and disarm it."

Montana ran toward the staircase leading below. "Mica, get Duff and Sawyer up here. Now! Take the lounge, helm and deck. Look in and under everything."

"I'm going with you below," Quentin said.

As Montana ran for the stairs, he said over his shoulder, "Kate, if he moves, shoot him! And in case we don't make it out of this alive, I think I love you."

He leaped to the bottom of the stairs and ran straight for the galley, searching through anything large enough to hold a dirty bomb. Hell, he didn't know what a dirty bomb even looked like. All the while, he counted down. One thousand one, one thousand two…marking each second of the remaining minute.

When he didn't find anything in the galley, he threw open the door marked Engine Room. He stood for five seconds, staring at all the parts that made up a yacht engine. Finally, his gaze landed on what he thought was a toolbox, but it was duct taped to the wall. On closer inspection, he noticed an electronic timer displaying the number 21, then 20, then 19…

"Found it!" Montana shouted, and dropped to his knees, studying the contraption, his heart slamming against his ribs, his mind racing through a thousand different scenarios. As a SEAL, he'd been trained in demolitions. Some bombs were set up to explode if tampered with. If this was one of them, he could doom them and all of DC to death if he pulled the wrong wire.

The numbers clicked by…11…10…9…8 and he was no closer to figuring it out. When it came down to 5…4…3 he grabbed all the wires leading from the clock to the bomb and yanked as hard as he could. Three of the five came loose, but the clock didn't stop. In the last second, Montana sent a prayer heavenward, ripped out the last two wires, took what he thought might be his last breath and held it.

Quentin slid to a stop beside him, breathing hard. "You found it?"

Montana nodded and held up a handful of wires, unable to say anything.

Quentin looked from Montana to the bomb and back to Montana, then dropped to his knees and bent over, his shoulders shaking.

Montana frowned. "Hey, dude, I think we're okay. It didn't explode."

Without looking up, Quentin reached out and touched Montana's arm, his shoulders still shaking. "Oh, Montana. I wish you could have seen your face." When Quentin raised his head, his own face was wreathed in a huge smile and tears were running from his eyes. "I know I shouldn't laugh, but the expression on your face was the funniest thing I've ever seen." He bent again and his shoulders shook, the laughter making its way up to burst from his throat.

Montana stood, pulled his friend to his feet and suffered through a bone-crunching hug.

"Thanks, man. You saved our butts." Quentin rubbed the tears from his eyes and clapped his hand on Montana's back. "Let's go clean up the rest and call in the Feds. I'm sure they're going to want to dispose of the bomb."

Montana led the way up to the lounge, where Kate was applying zip ties to Carruthers's wrists and ankles, while Duff did the same with the computer guy.

"Mind telling us what's going on?" Lance said into Montana's ear. "We just got to the marina. Where are you guys?"

Montana glanced at Duff. "You want to fill him in and get this ball rolling? I'd like to get back to HQ by morning."

Kate stepped in front of him and held out her hand. "Care to take a stroll on the deck?"

Montana took her hand in his and held on tight. Together, they stepped through the sliding glass doors onto the deck. The clouds had completely cleared from the sky, and the lights of the capital shone like a brilliant crown.

Kate leaned against him. "Thanks."

"For what?" God, he loved her body resting against his. He couldn't wait to get her alone. And naked.

"For saving us and the city."

Montana shrugged. "All I did was pull a few wires."

She shook her head and held out her other hand. "Must have been a little bit more intense than that. You still have the wires in your hand."

He glanced down and laughed. She was right. He'd been so intent on keeping Kate and the rest of his friends alive, he didn't remember to put the mass of wires down.

Kate took them from his hand and laid them on the deck. Then she turned to face him. "About what you said before we were almost obliterated from the map… Did you mean it?"

Montana knew what he'd said, but now that they were going to live, he didn't know what it would mean to Kate. "Look, I don't want you to feel like you have to commit to anything or say anything you don't mean. All I want is the chance to see you again."

She nodded. "Fair enough. And if I decide there's something more than amazing sex between us, then what? How would a relationship between a CIA agent and a Navy SEAL ever work?"

"I could ask to be transferred to Little Creek in Virginia. It's a lot closer than Mississippi," he said, his hopes rising dangerously. He'd known Kate only a few days, and in that time frame they'd lived a lifetime. He knew what he wanted, but he'd need time with Kate to convince her she wanted the same.

"Why move to Little Creek? Your team is in Mississippi. You've been through so much with them."

He had, and it would be hard starting over on another team. "Kate, you're worth it. I'd rip the wires out of a thousand bombs to get to spend even one more day with you."

Tears welled in Kate's eyes. "Damn you, Ben."

His heart swelled at her use of his first name. "That's the first time you've called me Ben." He gathered her in his arms. She didn't pull away. Hell, maybe he had a chance with her.

"Damn you." She laid her hand on his chest and tears ran down her cheeks. "I didn't want to. But you're making me."

He chuckled, his chest filling with hope. He rested his forehead against hers. "Making you what?"

Kate raised her hand and cupped the back

of his neck. "You're making me fall in love with you."

Joy exploded inside him and he felt he could light up the sky with it. He tightened his arm around her waist and tipped her chin up to his. "Is that such a bad thing?"

"It's bad. Very bad." Kate leaned up on her toes and brushed his lips with hers. "I lose control when I'm around you."

"From my perspective, that's a very good thing. And kissing you is even better." He bent to take her lips in a heart-stopping, soul-defining kiss that only ended when the port authority's boat pulled up beside them and shone a spotlight on them. Even then, Montana didn't want to let go.

"Put your hands up and hold them high where we can see them."

Slowly, he released her and backed away. As he raised his hands, he said, "I surrender my heart to you, Kate McKenzie."

She smiled and raised her hands, as well. "And I surrender mine to you."

* * * * *

Don't miss the previous books
in Elle James's exciting
SEAL OF MY OWN *miniseries:*

NAVY SEAL TO DIE FOR
NAVY SEAL CAPTIVE
NAVY SEAL SURVIVAL

Available now from Harlequin Intrigue!

"With this ring, I thee fake wed. I promise to save your butt, should the need arise...again. And should you try anything without my permission, I promise to hurt you." Kate raised her brows. "Got it?"

He held up his hand. "Got it. I won't *try* anything without your permission." As Kate took his upraised hand and slipped the ring onto his finger, Montana muttered, "I don't *try*...I *do*."

Kate glared at him. "This marriage is fake. Don't forget that."

"Trust me. I won't." Montana leaned forward and pressed his lips to hers in a brief brush of a kiss.

A blast of electricity ripped through Kate, followed by heat, searing a path through her chest and down low in her belly. She pressed her fingers to her lips. "Why did you do that?"

"Only seemed fitting, after tying the knot." He winked, sending another rush of heat rushing through her veins. "Want me to take it back?"